LOST SOULS, SACRED CREATURES

*Lost Souls, Sacred Creature*s

THAMES RIVER PRESS
An imprint of Wimbledon Publishing Company Limited (WPC)
Another imprint of WPC is Anthem Press (www.anthempress.com)
First published in the United Kingdom in 2013 by
THAMES RIVER PRESS
75–76 Blackfriars Road
London SE1 8HA

www.thamesriverpress.com

Original title: *Soshinki*
Copyright © Juko Nishimura 1988
Originally published in Japan by Tokuma Shoten Publishing Co., Ltd.
English translation copyright © Jeffrey Hunter 2013

All rights reserved. No part of this publication may be reproduced
in any form or by any means without written permission of the publisher.

The moral rights of the author have been asserted in accordance
with the Copyright, Designs and Patents Act 1988.

All the characters and events described in this novel are imaginary
and any similarity with real people or events is purely coincidental.

A CIP record for this book is available from the British Library.

ISBN 978-0-85728-128-9

This title is also available as an eBook.

This book has been selected by the Japanese Literature Publishing Project (JLPP),
an initiative of the Agency for Cultural Affairs of Japan.

LOST SOULS, SACRED CREATURES

JUKO NISHIMURA

Translated by Jeffrey Hunter

THAMES RIVER PRESS

The Emaciated Cow Demon

1

The first person to notice the disappearance of Kikunogo was Cattle Husbandry Manager Taiichi Hiraga.

Ten heifers were housed in the barn.

They were choice, individually-raised cows.

The stockmen started work at 7:00 a.m. They all had lodgings on the farm, but according to their union contract, they were only on duty from 7:00 a.m. to 5:00 p.m.

It was before 6:00 a.m. when Hiraga made his rounds.

The choice, individually-raised heifers were scheduled to be delivered to the slaughterhouse in two days.

Matsuzaka Ranch, where Hiraga worked, was one of the few cattle operations in Japan raising large herds of Matsuzaka beef cows. They had more than four thousand head of Japanese cattle.

In that large herd, only ten had been selected for individual raising. But these were very special cattle. Your ordinary animal sold for between one and a half to two million yen, but these special heifers started at several million yen and, in some cases, might go up to nearly ten million yen. They were raised differently, and their meat was different.

They were the standard bearers of the Matsuzaka brand.

One of those heifers had disappeared.

At first Hiraga thought he'd counted wrong.

It was unthinkable that an animal should disappear, so he wasn't actually counting them. While he was checking on their condition, one at a time, prior to their delivery to the slaughterhouse, he somehow had the feeling that one heifer was missing.

2

He counted, and there were only nine.

That's impossible. He counted again. Nine, same as the first time.

Now Hiraga went pale.

He left the barn.

He looked out at the open fields of the ranch. There was a thin morning mist. No living thing was in sight. No, a few crows were hopping about. They were the only things moving.

The missing Kikunogo couldn't be out in the fields.

He went through all the barns. There were a dozen or so large barns with glass walls. About three hundred cattle were in each barn. Each barn cost more than ten million yen to build. They were all heated and environmentally controlled by computer-operated systems.

The barn for the choice heifers was especially well maintained. There was a lock on the door. There was no way Kikunogo could escape.

Hiraga stood there in a daze for a while.

Then suddenly, as if struck by something, he began to run.

6:40 a.m.

Hiraga discovered that Kikunogo had been stolen sometime during the night.

A small truck used to transport cattle was missing. Following the tire tracks, he found telltale signs that the truck had been driven off with a heifer in it.

Twenty minutes later, he figured out who had stolen Kikunogo.

It was Kōji Tendō, a young stockman who lived on the ranch.

Tendō was the only one who didn't show up for work at 7:00 a.m. The stockmen, learning of Kikunogo's disappearance, had all made an appearance.

Hiraga searched Tendō's room.

It was empty.

Reporting the theft to the Mie Prefectural Police, the Matsuzaka Ranch also formed its own search party. They sent more than twenty cars out looking for the truck.

9:00 a.m.

Hiraga was called into the office of the ranch owner, Yasuo Asakura.

"Still haven't found it?"

Asakura was about sixty years old. He was fat, but not jovial—a tightly-wound type. His face was white with rage.

"Not so far…" Hiraga mumbled.

"This isn't what I expect from you. You hired a cattle thief. This is highly unprofessional."

Asakura was always quick to point out others' failings. He glared at Hiraga accusingly.

Apologizing abjectly, Hiraga excused himself.

He went to the barn.

Hiraga had been working for Matsuzaka Ranch for twelve years. He'd been there in the days when the farm specialized in raising heifers individually. He'd been recognized as a top-rated heifer stockman. He'd devoted half his life to raising Matsuzaka beef, and was now in his mid-forties.

He couldn't deny that though he knew how to judge cows, he was no judge of people.

But no one would ever have expected a heifer to be stolen. Even if you tried, there was no way to get it off the ranch. You could bring a truck, but the heifer wouldn't get on to it voluntarily. It knew very well that the truck was taking it to the slaughterhouse. You would have to push it in from the rear. It would resist, planting its feet. It would shake its head back and forth and low mournfully.

You would have to set a ramp up to the truck bed, cover it with straw matting so the heifer wouldn't slip, and pull from the front and push from the back to load the heifer. And only an experienced stockman could get it to do this.

No one would go through all that to steal a cow.

It was next to impossible to lead a cow away. The Matsuzaka heifers were raised in a special way to fatten them up.

Hogs were raised by keeping them in narrow pens and letting them eat continuously. The pen was too narrow for the animal to even turn around. They put on weight very quickly, but their bones never developed properly. If you let them out of their pens, they couldn't take more than a few steps. The same with broiler chickens.

A similar method was used for Matsuzaka beef. Every effort was made to keep the bones delicate. The idea was to boost the yield. If you let them walk, they easily broke a bone. If they tripped and fell, it was all over.

In short, it was impossible to steal one.

And then, say you did somehow steal one, you'd never find a buyer. No slaughterhouse would take the heifer. If you brought it to one, you'd be arrested on the spot.

Since the very idea of stealing one of the heifers was so unthinkable, Hiraga had never bothered to try to prevent it.

Hiraga called Hideo Hironaka, who was working in a barn, to come outside.

"If you know anything, Hidé, now's the time to tell me."

It was the second time he'd asked Hidé about the incident.

Hideo Hironaka was the oldest stockman on the Matsuzaka Ranch. He was nearly sixty. Everyone called him Hidé. He was a taciturn man. The reason he rarely spoke was that he was clumsy with words. He was short and scrawny. He wasn't the kind who called attention to himself. People didn't know much about him. In the old days, people may have known him better, but now no one was interested. He had no wife or children. He was just an old stockman living on the ranch.

Three years ago, at Hidé's request, Hiraga had hired Kōji Tendō, who'd stolen Kikunogo. The boy was a distant relative, his parents had died, and he had nowhere to go. He didn't need a salary at the start; he'd be happy with food, clothing, and a roof over his head.

Hiraga couldn't refuse Hidé, and so he hired the then fifteen-year-old Kōji Tendō.

"I'm so sorry…" said Hidé, lowering his head. His face and his hands were tinged the brown color of manure from decades of cleaning up the shit and piss of cattle.

"Stop repeating yourself," said Hiraga roughly. "If that's all you've got to say, I'll come right out with it: at seven hundred kilos, Tendō couldn't have loaded Kikunogo onto a truck all by himself. It's impossible. Someone helped him. The police will eventually find out. But I want to know first. Who helped him steal Kikunogo, and why?"

Hidé was silent.

"Hidé," said Hiraga, lowering his voice, "Hidé, you helped him, didn't you?"

"Me? I'd never do something like that…" Hidé shook his head slightly, without lifting his head.

Hiraga gave up his cross examination.

From a common sense standpoint, it would have been impossible for Hidé and Tendō to load Kikunogo on the truck by themselves anyway. Even someone like Hidé, who knew cattle so well.

And there was nothing for him to gain by assisting in the theft.

No one stole something without a motive. The same would hold true for the other stockmen.

"As you know, the day after tomorrow, Kikunogo was scheduled…" started Hiraga, then he fell silent.

Finishing his sentence wouldn't have made any difference.

Kikunogo was scheduled to be shipped off to Tokyo the day after tomorrow. A major department store had bought it as a live heifer. The final price would be decided after it was butchered and the quality of the meat's marbling was known, but it was expected to bring about six million yen. Matsuzaka Ranch was confident that its meat would be a work of art. When butchered, the beef would sell for about ten thousand yen a kilo. After going through the distribution system, it would be three times that, or thirty thousand yen a kilo. Three thousand yen for a hundred grams.

The department store was buying Kikunogo as a live heifer, so its meat wouldn't go through the distribution system. Their only cost would be the butchering. Their plan was to sell the choicest Matsuzaka beef at a special retail price.

The Matsuzaka Ranch is world famous for its choice Matsuzaka beef.

Most of it is bought as gifts. As December rolls around, lines form throughout Japan in search of choice Matsuzaka beef to give as gifts to favored customers and bosses.

Kikunogo had been born a pedigreed Tajima cow and specially raised for that very purpose.

Now Kikunogo had been stolen by Tendō.

Hiraga looked at his watch. It was 10:20 a.m.

With a dark expression he looked at Hidé's still-bowed head, and turned on his heel.

The situation was hopeless.

No matter where Tendō tried to hide the seven-hundred-kilo Kikunogo, it would only end badly. There was a very high chance that the heifer would fall and break a leg. If he tried to hide it in the mountains, they'd have a hard time bringing it safely back. If it broke a leg it was as good as dead. A heifer that died anywhere but the slaughterhouse would have to be disposed of as waste matter.

November 18. Weak sunlight, a sign of approaching winter, washed over the fields.

2

Kikunogo's whereabouts were not discovered that day.

The Mie Prefectural Police set up a broad dragnet, but to no avail.

November 19, the next day.

Halfway along National Highway 42 from Matsuzaka City to Kīnagashimachō is Ōdaichō. It's about twenty kilometers from Matsuzaka. The stolen truck was found abandoned on the outskirts of Ōdaichō.

The Matsuzaka Police Department dispatched several detectives.

A search team from Matsuzaka Ranch also headed for Ōdaichō.

The national highway runs parallel to the Kisei Line. The Miyagawa river flows nearby the highway.

It's a mountainous area.

The search began, focusing on the area around the abandoned truck. One road ran through the mountains from there to Iinan County, and another prefectural road went to Oku Ise Miyagawa Kyo Prefectural Park on the border with Nara Prefecture.

The general supposition was that they hadn't gotten far from where the truck was abandoned. The police and the Matsuzaka Ranch search team visited the settlements in the area.

A policeman in late middle age, stationed at the police box near the Matsuzaka Ranch, had been included as a member of the Matsuzaka Police team.

His name was Senji Nakamichi.

Borrowing a bicycle from the Ōdaichō head police box, Nakamichi rode around the area. Though winter was approaching, he broke a sweat as he cycled from village to village. He had to keep wiping away his perspiration with a hand towel.

As he rode, he thought about what could have motivated Tendō to steal Kikunogo. It was a question for which he could find no good answer. No matter which way you looked at it, there was no profit in it for him. If he stole the heifer knowing there was no profit in it, the only thing left was emotion.

Was there some kind of sentimental attachment between the heifer Kikunogo and Kōji Tendō? That was the question. Maybe he took the heifer because he didn't want to see it killed.

Nakamichi posed that question to the people at Matsuzaka Ranch. Their answer was no. There were four thousand cattle on the Matsuzaka Ranch. They were precisely managed by the staff based on the most detailed calculations. There were about thirty stockmen. Thirty stockmen had to care for four thousand cattle. It was a ridiculous question.

It was true that Kōji Tendō was in charge of the care of the choice heifers. Kikunogo had been purchased from Tajima at about the time that the young Tendō started working at the ranch. He must have been familiar with the animal. But that was true not just of Kikunogo, but the other nine heifers as well. And Kōji Tendō was responsible for the care of cattle other than the choice heifers. The fact was that each stockman looked after more than a hundred cattle.

It was unthinkable that a stockman should come to have feelings for a heifer; it was laughable, impossible.

Matsuzaka Ranch categorically rejected the possibility. They'd said the same thing to the press.

Of course the press came running when it got out that a boy had run off with a Matsuzaka heifer worth six million yen. The reporters peppered the ranch mercilessly with questions.

Was Tendō's theft of Kikunogo a silent protest directed at the mighty Matsuzaka Ranch?

A protest against low stockmen's wages, inhumane husbandry methods, dosing the animals with antibiotics—that sort of thing?

There were elements of truth in all these accusations. Matsuzaka Ranch enforced a policy of complete secrecy. They refused to allow anyone to inspect their barns. They wouldn't even allow access to the prefectural instructors. One reason was fear of contamination.

Another reason was the desire to prevent their secret fattening methods from leaking out.

Matsuzaka cattle are not actually born in Matsuzaka. They're Tajima cattle, bred in the Mikata County region of Hyōgo Prefecture. Tajima cattle are regarded as the best of the Japanese Black breed. All the calves born there are registered with nose prints to identify them. Their pedigrees go back seven or eight generations.

Matsuzaka is just the place where Tajima cattle are fattened for market. There are supposed to be all kinds of secrets to this fattening process. Giving them beer to drink and rubbing them down with *shōchū* are part of it, as is the use of antibiotics and other supplements in their feed.

But these days there's not really much that's secret about how Matsuzaka cattle are fattened. The methods are all widely known. Moreover, individual farmers also raise Matsuzaka cattle. Always eager to improve their methods, they hold annual Matsuzaka cattle shows to advance the breed, and choose the best specimens. Several years ago the winning heifer in one of those shows sold for twelve million yen.

The cattle of the Matsuzaka Ranch aren't special because of some secret fattening methods; they're superior because they're each raised individually. The Matsuzaka Ranch staff are pros at the fattening process, so they're not allowed to take part in the cattle shows. Only farmers who are raising Matsuzaka heifers on the side can participate. That's the purpose of a breed-promotion association.

Since Matsuzaka Ranch cattle aren't shown, no one sees them. Their fattening methods are a mystery, too. But the Matsuzaka Ranch buys most of the prize-winning cows in the shows. Then they sell them, together with their own individually-raised heifers, under the prestigious brand name of Matsuzaka beef.

As a result, consumers immediately think of the Matsuzaka Ranch when they hear the words "Matsuzaka beef." It was no exaggeration to say the control of the brand "Matsuzaka beef" rested in the hands of the Matsuzaka Ranch.

It was, simply put, a very clever business strategy.

As a result, they were disliked by the farmers, who poured their energies into raising their cows and discovering the best ways to fatten them for market, and in the end all their efforts only increased the prestige of the Matsuzaka Ranch.

But more than anything, they resented the ranch's policy of secrecy.

They must be using drugs to fatten their cows—many of the local people had bad things to say about Matsuzaka Ranch.

That was the backstory prompting the reporters' questions.

Matsuzaka Ranch vehemently denied such charges.

Nakamichi had been thinking about all this.

The answer given by the Matsuzaka Ranch people seemed right. It would be impossible for a stockman in charge of over one hundred cows to come to have special feelings for just one animal. Most of his time would be spent shoveling manure. A cow passes two kilos of excrement at a time, a total of six kilos a day. With four thousand cows, that's an enormous amount of cow shit. Today they dry it in kilns and sell it as fertilizer. That was another part of their job.

What, then, was the reason that Kōji Tendō stole Kikunogo?

He didn't get it.

He couldn't be expected to get it.

Kōji Tendō was born on a little island in the Inland Sea. He'd lived there until he entreated upon Hideo Hironaka who worked at the Matsuzaka Ranch. He was an unfortunate lad, said Hidé. His mother had disappeared several years before he came to work at the ranch, and he'd been living with his father. His father was a fisherman. One day he went out to sea, ran into a sudden storm, and died.

Hidé, a distant relation, was the only one to whom he could turn.

Kōji was said to be a boy of few words, like Hidé—though Nakamichi didn't know that.

"I don't understand his motive," Nakamichi thought to himself as he pedaled the bicycle.

Nakamichi wasn't an investigator. He was an ordinary police officer, just about to retire, serving in a police box; he knew he was no one special. He was almost completely ignorant of investigative procedures. But the one thing he did know is that no one steals something without a motive.

There is a motive. There is, but Matsuzaka Ranch is keeping it under wraps. There must be something going on at the Matsuzaka Ranch that they don't want people to find out about.

He felt that the matter was going to end badly. The combination of the six-million-yen prize heifer Kikunogo, the quiet, unfortunate boy, and the secretive Matsuzaka Ranch—it didn't bode well.

The trail of Kōji Tendō and Kikunogo still undiscovered, the day came to its end.

Nakamichi took the train back to Matsuzaka.

November 20.

It was before noon on the third day since the theft of Kikunogo.

A man claiming to be a reporter from the *Daily Meat* called on Hiraga Taiichi at the Matsuzaka Ranch.

He was young. His business card gave his name as Hiroshi Inoue. He seemed around thirty, and he had long hair reaching his shoulders. His complexion was sallow and his eyes shifty.

"It's such a strange story that I'd like to cover it…" he started in a low voice, keeping his eyes averted.

"I have no comment. It's just as we said to the papers." Hiraga looked noticeably weary.

"They say that Kikunogo was worth six million yen."

"Yes, that's about right I guess," he replied offhandedly.

"Kikunogo was roughly seven hundred kilos. It seems to me that it would be impossible for the boy Kōji Tendō to load it into a truck all by himself."

"Yes, just as we said to the papers…" Hiraga was irritated. He didn't have time to stand here talking with a reporter from an industry rag. Most of them were useless anyway.

And this guy exuded a distinct smarminess.

Hiraga didn't like the way that the news media were using the theft of Kikunogo to pry into the internal affairs of the Matsuzaka Ranch.

"I have a theory. Would you like to hear it?" He still refused to look Hiraga in the eye.

"And what might that be?"

"Tendō got Kikunogo into the truck without anyone's help. The reason is, Kikunogo trusted the boy. They say a cow knows when it's about to be slaughtered. This one was scheduled to be carted off to the slaughterhouse in two days. Tendō whispered to her, 'I won't kill you. I won't let them kill you,' and told it they were running away."

Hiraga remained silent.

"Kikunogo was glad to follow Tendō. But running off with a seven-hundred-kilo heifer is no simple matter. The animal could quickly break a leg. The choice, individually reared cows, however, unlike the rest of the Matsuzaka cows, get plenty of exercise and sunlight when they're calves. This strengthens their bones. So that they can support their enormous bulk later on. There are various criteria for choosing breeding cattle in Tajima. First is the quality of the meat in the animal's pedigree. Then you look for a broad back and good ribs, a refined face, a broad lower chest, a projecting tail joint—all sorts of qualities, including thick, strong leg joints. Am I right?"

"What are you getting at?"

"What I'm getting at is that Kikunogo got into the truck on its own. Tendō had a special affection for Kikunogo, and at night he used to exercise it. To prepare for their escape. All cows weep when they are sent off to the slaughterhouse. They cry. It's very sad."

"Give me a break," said Hiraga, his voice quavering.

"In other words, Tendō didn't want Kikunogo, whom he'd worked so hard to raise, to suffer that fate. Matsuzaka cattle aren't real cattle. They're changed into something else. You raise them in a special way, don't you? In the process of raising a perfectly healthy Tajima cow, Tendō was forced by the ranch to dump antibiotics and other additives into its feed. He came to understand the cow's misery, and he couldn't stand it any longer. With the pure heart of a boy, he wanted the world to know how these cows are raised to be killed, don't you think?"

Inoue raised his shifty eyes and gave Hiraga one quick glance before lowering them again.

Hiraga said nothing.

3

November 21.

    The fourth day after Kikunogo's theft.

    Early morning. Matsuzaka Ranch informs the Matsuzaka Office of the Mie Prefecture Police that they are dropping all charges. The police are suspicious. Kōji Tendō, after all, has stolen a six-million-yen cow. This is not a matter that can be resolved by simply dropping the charges. The police inquire further.

    Mastusaka Ranch responds.

    While it's unclear what Tendō's motivation for taking Kikunogo is, pursuing the matter further is certain to result in the cow's death. This is not the intent of Matsuzaka Ranch. Hard as it may be to imagine, if somehow, hypothetically speaking, Tendō has some emotional connection to Kikunogo, the ranch wishes to present the cow to him. This will prevent the senseless death of Kikunogo as well as turning a young man with his entire future still ahead of him into a criminal. As such, the ranch wishes the police to understand that the case of theft involving the ranch and Tendō has been amicably resolved.

    The Matsuzaka Police were silent.

    Since the victim had decided to repudiate being victimized, there was no crime to investigate.

    The investigation into the theft was canceled.

An article to that effect appeared in the evening paper.

    After outlining the latest developments, it included a message from Matsuzaka Ranch to Kōji Tendō: If Tendō had special feelings for Kikunogo, the ranch presented the animal to him. He could bring it back and care for it at the ranch or take it wherever he pleased. We are proud of producing Matsuzaka beef; that's what we want you to understand.

Senji Namakichi, back again at his job in the police box, read the article in the paper as he was having a drink over dinner.

    This was odd. He tilted his head to the side in perplexity. He had known about the dropped charges. An order to halt the investigation had been issued. Everyone was talking about it, at the police box and on his beat. Most welcomed this development.

It would have been tough going from village to village, mountain to mountain, looking for the boy and the cow. And if they caught him, it was only a theft, after all.

And, as the Matsuzaka Ranch said, chasing after them was likely to result in the animal's death.

The general response was that this wise and magnanimous approach was just what you'd expect from a class operation like the Matsuzaka Ranch.

Senji Nakamichi seemed to be the only person who didn't see it that way.

There had to be a reason for letting a six-million-yen heifer go. Anyway, that's what he thought.

But by the time he put down the newspaper, he'd forgotten about it. What Nakamichi thought about it didn't change anything. He could go and ask about it at the Matsuzaka Ranch, but they'd ignore him. It was a big ranch, the proprietor of the prestigious Matsuzaka beef brand.

The next day.

Nakamichi went to headquarters to make his report. While he was there, he heard a strange thing. Yesterday and today, an investigative team from Matsuzaka Ranch had been out asking questions on the outskirts of Ōdaichō.

"We're presenting you with Kikunogo. You're free to keep it wherever you like." But they're still looking for her. "If we chase after them it will result in the animal's death." Though they told the public that isn't their intent, they're still on the trail.

He didn't get it.

Late that afternoon, Nakamichi went to visit a farmer named Nishino who raised Matsuzaka cows. He was a personal friend.

"What do you think is going on?" he asked.

"Who knows? They're so damn secretive about everything," said Nishino with a bitter smile.

"I wonder." He sat down on the porch and took out a cigarette.

"Maybe they think that they have a better chance of getting Kikunogo back alive if they're the only ones doing the searching. After all, she's worth six million yen. Or..." Nishino hesitated.

"Or?" The fiery cockscomb blossoms in the yard were so intense that they seemed to color the air.

"You're allowed to give cows antibiotics for the first six months, but it's forbidden to mix them in with the feed after that, except for medical treatment. But the fact is they fatten up faster if you give them antibiotics. And they don't show up in tests for residual traces, so if you give them on the sly, no one's the wiser. This is just a rumor, but they say that the stomach lining of Matsuzaka Ranch cattle is usually so thin that it isn't good enough for grilling. At least that's what I've heard. I don't know whether it's true or not, but…"

A conflicted expression passed over Nishino's face.

"I wonder."

"No one enjoys sending a cow they've raised to the slaughterhouse. After all, you've put so much time and effort into the animal day after day…"

Nakamichi said nothing.

"If the kid took Kikunogo away because he felt sorry for her, he's also making a protest against all of us. If the story attracts too much attention, it'll have a negative effect on Matsuzaka beef as a whole. So maybe that's what the Matsuzaka Ranch is thinking. It's true, depending on how you look at things, that the way Matsuzaka cows are raised is not really right."

Nishino paused for a moment, then added: "But no matter how you raise them, they end up being eaten all the same. In the end…"

And there he stopped.

Nakamichi was looking at the cockscomb flowers.

He wasn't absolutely certain, but he thought he had a general grasp of the problem.

How had Kōji Tendō managed to get the heifer into the truck all by himself? Where was he hiding now, five days after making off with this Matsuzaka cow who could easily have broken its leg merely by tripping over something? These were the unsolved riddles.

And, though responsible for the care of over a hundred cattle, why had Kōji Tendō come to have special feelings for Kikunogo—that was a mystery, too.

But he had a vague idea of why the Matsuzaka Ranch had withdrawn its charges and canceled its claim of damages against Kōji Tendō.

The Matsuzaka Ranch might be afraid of damaging the brand "Matsuzaka beef." If they pursued the boy, eventually the boy would turn on them. Kōji Tendō was said to be the quiet type. If that normally reserved boy decided to go on the attack, the Matsuzaka Ranch might find itself in a very uncomfortable situation.

People knew that Matsuzaka cows were fattened by restricting their mobility and keeping their bone structure weak. Every possible step was taken to increase their bulk. They were given beer to stimulate their appetite and rubbed down with *shōchū*. This was all true, but it might not be everything. You were allowed to give them antibiotics for the first six months of life, but after that it was prohibited. Since testing didn't pick up any residual traces, they might continue to receive antibiotics after that cut off date.

If arrested, the boy might spill that to the police.

The question was, how would the public react to the boy's exposé about Matsuzaka Ranch?

The mighty Matsuzaka Ranch might well be defeated by this one quiet boy.

That's why they sheathed their sword and withdrew the charges.

Nakamichi sighed softly to himself.

Where, he wondered, was Kōji Tendō hiding? Did he steal Kikunogo because he intended to reveal the secrets of the Matsuzaka Ranch? Did he plan on being pursued by the police and the ranch, and was he now waiting somewhere for the right moment, when public opinion had come over to his side?

Was he simply outraged by the unnatural fattening methods used to produce Matsuzaka beef?

Or was there something else that was driving Kōji Tendō to keep Kikunogo from being killed?

Nakamichi wished he could talk to Kōji Tendō. He wanted to know what the boy was thinking. He wanted to know what in his past had driven him to do what he'd done.

4

Winter had come to the Takami Highlands.

A thin blanket of clouds rested on Tsubonegatake Peak.

The wind blew through the brown grass.

A cow stood in the wind, grazing.

A boy in jeans and high boots watched over it.

It was Kōji Tendō and Kikunogo.

Kōji Tendō wore an expression resembling melancholy. There was a bewildered look in his eyes.

It was the ninth day since he'd stolen Kikunogo.

He was sure that he'd be safe once he made it into the mountains. He drove as fast as he could from Matsuzaka. He headed west on National Highway 166. The Wakayama Road. He reached Iitakachō. Turning right, he arrived in the Takami Highlands.

There were several abandoned villages in the area. He knew from having hiked around there several times on his days off.

Kōji tethered Kikunogo in the mountains, then turned back around. He drove over one mountain range to Ōdaichō and left the truck there.

He was certain the search teams would never come this far.

He had no fear of being caught, but he was very much afraid of how he'd survive. He had nothing to eat. After deciding to run off with Kikunogo, he'd purchased some canned and packaged foods. He had managed to put aside nearly one hundred thousand yen from his meager salary, and that had all gone towards a sleeping bag and food.

And now he was running out of food.

Soon he'd have nothing to eat.

His food supply was running out at the same rate, it seemed, that the weather grew colder. He could hear the footsteps of winter approaching.

Kōji looked at Kikunogo.

She had rapidly grown thinner. She'd probably gone down from seven hundred to six hundred kilos. It was a stunning transformation.

Kōji wasn't worried about her getting thin. When she entered the fattening period, she was given all the food she would eat. It was called concentrated feeding. A rich mixture of barleycorn, wheat bran, and soy meal, along with water were constantly passing in front of her on a conveyor belt. Top-quality dried grass was always available.

The barn was kept dark and quiet so the cows could focus on eating.

They spent all their time doing so. And they were forced to drink beer to make them eat even more. Some forced the cows to drink sweet saké. In the final fattening period, they were given *mochi* rice and brown sugar. *Shōchū* was sprayed on their bodies and they were massaged. They were fed salt and made to consume fifty grams of calcium a day to improve the color of their meat.

If they didn't fatten up with all this, something was wrong.

In the last days, most cows gained about 0.7 kilos a day.

There were like machines, thought Kōji. There was no life left in them. The barn was occupied by high-tech machines called "cows." They were fed rich feed, huge amounts of antibiotics, vitamins, and lysine. They were given dried grass, beer, *shōchū,* sweet saké, and brown sugar.

They were even given yeast. This was to stop their manure from stinking. The ranchers said it was to prevent pollution.

All these ingredients were crammed down the throats of the "cow machines," and they converted them into meat.

It was sad to watch.

Now Kikunogo's flesh, which was really nothing more than the accumulated residue of poisons pumped into her, was quickly melting away.

Cows are very sensitive. They have very keen senses of smell and hearing, and they have a well-developed awareness of their fate. When they're put in a truck and carted to the slaughterhouse, they can drop fifty kilos of meat in a day. No doubt, this is partly due to stress, but partly to fear of their impending death.

Kōji couldn't help but think that, having all that food pumped into them, the cows with their keen olfactory sense sniffed out just what it was they were being fattened up for.

Now Kikunogo was regaining her life. She was growing thin because she was shedding the poisons that had accumulated in her body. Eventually her flesh would return to the real flesh of a cow— firm and strong. The flabby marbled fat that had been forced on her frame by humans would disappear and all that would remain was the powerful muscle she needed to survive.

Kōji walked up to Kikunogo.

He started to rub her body with a straw rope. When he approached he smelled that uniquely musty bovine scent, almost like something burning.

You never smelled this in the barn. Their natural scent extinguished by the yeast in their food and the *shōchū* rubbed into their skin, the cows in the barn had lost the normal odor that all cows possess as an essential part of their bovine nature.

Kikunogo ate the dried grass voraciously.

"You must be hungry," said Kōji.

There was no barleycorn, wheat bran, or soy meal here. Just dried grass, with a few green shoots remaining here and there. Kikunogo ate everything within reach. She devoured every blade of fresh grass, which she'd never had access to until now.

In fattening cows, it's important to stretch their stomachs. Kikunogo's stomach was enormously distended. It would be hard to fill it with grass alone.

That made Kōji sad. For a moment the doubt arose in his mind—maybe Kikunogo wished she were back in the barn. Though she spent the entire day walking through the fields eating every weed and stem of grass, she kept losing weight.

Though he knew she was returning to her natural form, still, it was hard to watch.

Winter would be here soon.

Rubbing Kikunogo's back, Kōji looked up at the mountains. There were signs of snow on the peaks already. He was afraid when he thought about what he'd do if it snowed. If the meager remaining dried grass were covered with snow, he'd have no way to feed Kikunogo.

And not only Kikunogo. Kōji himself was running out of food for the days ahead.

Had he been too hasty?

Kōji rejected that thought. He hadn't been hasty. By the time he learned the date that the choice, individually-fattened cows would be sent to slaughter, there wasn't a moment to lose. It was all he could do just to escape with Kikunogo. He hadn't foreseen that this would happen, but there had been no choice.

He was neither overly hasty nor overly cautious.

But he had nowhere to go. Until his father's death, he had fished with him. He had no choice.

Kōji was unable to bear the thought of Kikunogo being dragged up the ramp to the truck, weeping and lowing in fear.

The wind rose.

Kikunogo continued her eager grazing.

Kōji stopped rubbing her and looked vaguely at the sky beyond her back.

Distant memories materialized in the air.

Kōji was raising a Japanese Black calf.

In those days, most people could no longer raise Japanese Black cows. The island was small and the fields terraced, and you couldn't use motorized farm equipment. The only way to plow the fields was with oxen, but the island residents had given up farming. You made more money as a hired laborer or a fisherman.

If anyone kept a cow, it would be a dairy cow.

Kōji's family was poor. His father was not a resourceful man. He could only manage by both fishing and, when he wasn't fishing, farming. By farming, he was able to grow his own food.

Taking care of the cow was Kōji's job. Before leaving for elementary school, he had to get up early and cut grass for the cow—enough to last all day.

When he couldn't find grass, he drove the cow to a farm at the north end of the island and let her eat in the pasture. After school, he went to get the cow and bring her back home.

The cow would have eaten her fill of grass and be sleeping. There were no other cows on the farm. A few years earlier, there had been a herd of cows, but now there was only Kōji's cow, Chibi.

Kōji would climb the fence surrounding the spacious pasture and whistle, and Chibi would come running from wherever she was.

Since she was only a calf, she must have been lonely. He'd come up to Chibi and play with her, pretending to lock horns with her.

She was very obedient. When Kōji called Chibi from a distance, she would raise his muzzle and reply.

By the time Kōji was a junior high school student, Chibi had grown up. Kōji was very proud of Chibi's long, sharp horns. When Kōji took Chibi into the woods, she used to play by attacking trees and bushes with her horns. There weren't even any stray dogs on the island. In spite of having no enemies to defend herself against, Chibi was always sharpening her horns until they gleamed.

She allowed Kōji to ride her.

Once he graduated junior high, Kōji would have to help his father. Kōji was the only boy in the island who wouldn't go on to attend high school. During junior high, his schoolmates were busy studying for high school entrance exams, but Kōji didn't feel particularly bad that he wouldn't be joining them.

He wasn't good at school. Problems that his classmates solved easily remained a mystery to him.

He had no second thoughts about following in his fathers footsteps as a fisherman. He expected to, and to use Chibi to plow their fields when he wasn't fishing.

Chibi was only sick once. She began to moo sadly in the middle of the night. Kōji woke up and went out to the barn. Chibi was lying down. Her stomach was conspicuously swollen. She was panting, as if in pain. Worried, Kōji went to call the cattle broker. The broker was a large man with one eye. Now he worked as the captain on a boat that sailed the Inland Sea. He had to give up being a livestock broker since there were no more cattle on the island. Even though it was the middle of the night, he wasn't angry. In fact, he seemed happy about it. He came to look at Chibi.

It was cattle bloat. Gasses had accumulated in her stomach. The swelling pressed on her heart, so it was extremely painful. The livestock broker told Kōji to gently massage Chibi's stomach with a straw rope.

The livestock broker went home, called a veterinarian on the larger island nearby and woke him up, and went there in his boat to bring the veterinarian over.

The vet released the gas with a needle.

It took more than three hours for the vet to get there. Rubbing Chibi's stomach with the rope, Kōji kept repeating, "Don't die, don't die." Chibi just lay there. Tears rose in her huge eyes. Seeing the tears, Kōji thought Chibi was dying.

After the gas had been released, Chibi pressed her muzzle into Kōji. Kōji embraced her large face and scratched the thick bone between the animal's eyes. While he did that, Chibi rested there quietly.

When Kōji was in his second year of junior high, his mother, thirty-nine years old, left home.

Someone in the village had seen her in the woods in the naked embrace of a young man in the village.

His father punched her, and they had a violent fight.

The next day his mother left the island. She disappeared while Kōji was at school. She didn't leave a message. She had always been a cold woman. She held his father in contempt. She hated being poor.

He'd heard that she'd gone to Ōsaka, but Kōji hated his mother for cheating on his father.

One day three months after she'd left, Kōji returned home to find the livestock dealer leading Chibi away. His father was there, too.

When he learned that his father had sold Chibi to be slaughtered, Kōji was aghast. He had never dreamed this would happen.

He cried and asked his father not to do it. He promised to quit school the next day and help his father. I'll do whatever you ask, he pleaded tearfully, Just don't sell Chibi. It was like selling a family member. And not only that, she was going to be killed and eaten.

But his father flatly refused. After Kōji's mother had run away, his father had changed. He was often angry, and had begun drinking heavily, often to the point of being hungover the next day.

The livestock dealer, his one eye shining eagerly, led Chibi away.

Chibi resisted. She refused to move. The dealer pulled her nose ring hard enough to wrench her muzzle off, but still she refused to move. As she was being pulled, she looked at Kōji. Chibi's eyes were filled with tears. The tears fell to the ground. She continued to look at Kōji.

Kōji screamed, "Kill him with your horns!"

Chibi moaned. It was the first time Kōji had ever heard this sound, a sad call that seemed a plea for help. It was different than her usual voice. Kōji's vision was blurred with tears. Blearily, he could see his father beating Chibi on the rump with a stick.

Chibi began to walk.

Her mooing trailed off into the distance.

Clinging to the barn door, Kōji wept. His body shook. He couldn't stop shaking.

I'll kill myself! he said to himself.

Kōji didn't kill himself.

It was his father who died.

At the end of that year, Kōji and his father went out to fishing for crabs. Crabs sold for a high price. You could only catch them in the winter, on moonless nights. They hid on nights when the moon was out. Since they were such a profitable catch, people went out for them even when the sea was a bit rough.

As it was that night. After midnight, a strong wind began to blow. His father decided to call it quits. If they stayed any longer, they might encounter trouble.

Kōji held the outboard motor and his father the rudder. On their way back, his father began to bail out the water that had splashed into the boat with the spray. Kōji held the rudder. While his father was standing in the middle of the boat, Kōji quickly turned the rudder sharply over a high wave.

His father screamed and disappeared into the sea.

The next day his corpse washed up on the beach.

Kōji looked down at the corpse coldly.

Having found a live-in job at the Matsuzaka Ranch through his distant relative Hideo Hironaka, Kōji went pale when he saw one of the cows that had been brought from Tajima to become choice, individually-raised heifers.

The calf's face was a dead match for Chibi's. And the calf looked directly at Kōji with her cute, round eyes and bleated.

Kōji trembled. It seemed that Chibi, who had been killed and eaten, had been reborn. Even her voice was the same.

He knew nothing about the theory of reincarnation. He didn't even know the word. He just thought that Chibi had been reborn as this cow Kikunogo and had reappeared in his life. It was the only possibility.

5

The abandoned village was enveloped by the cold rain.

It had been falling since yesterday. Kōji Tendō was lying up against Kikunogo's belly, sitting on the rotting tatami matting in an empty house.

It was the fourteenth day since he'd stolen Kikunogo.

His food had run out yesterday.

He had no money.

Kikunogo's belly was warm. She was warm, but so thin as to be unrecognizable from fourteen days ago. Her hip bones were starting to protrude. At the same time, she was much stronger. She was lean. All of the meat that her keepers at Matsuzaka Ranch had worked so hard to put on her was gone.

It was an illusion. That flabby, marbled meat was nothing but a man-made illusion. Man-made things quickly disappear. When you thought about how quickly it disappeared, you had to ask yourself just what that prized Matsuzaka beef actually was.

It was nothing other than a mad delusion—a fantastical red-and-white pattern woven from overly rich feed, masses of antibiotics and pharmaceuticals, beer, *shōchū*, sweet saké, brown sugar, and *mochi* rice.

Kikunogo was chewing her cud in a leisurely fashion. She had never experienced such deprivation and want in all her life. Her distended stomach seemed to be craving her former heavy, rich feed.

The sound of her chewing her cud seemed like an expression of discontent. When cattle are given rich feed, they spend less time chewing their cud. Such feed is easily digested, and they have no need to re-chew it. When you give them feed with a high fiber content, they spend more time chewing their cud. Their stomach is more active. It was the sound of the stomach lining that had become so thin from rich feed and antibiotics, rejuvenating itself.

"How are you, Chibi?" said Kōji in a lifeless voice. From the first time they'd met, Kōji had called Kikunogo "Chibi." Kikunogo had come to recognize it as her name. From the time she was a calf, Kōji had taken her out of the barn in the middle of the night to exercise her. He wanted to make her legs strong. When he called out her name, she came running up to him, just like the old Chibi had.

"You must be unhappy, not having anything good to eat. Or is this better?"

Chibi went on chewing her cud.

"This is much better than being slaughtered. Even if you starve to death."

She might starve to death, but at least she was free. It was completely different from being slaughtered. Given the choice between suicide and execution, anyone would choose suicide.

If Chibi did starve to death, Kōji would be able to look at it as her natural destiny.

Why, he wondered, do people eat cows?

Chibi stood up.

"Where are you going? Chibi. You'll catch cold."

Chibi stepped down into the earthen entryway of the house and, waving her tail, walked out into the cold rain.

Kōji remained still. He watched Chibi go out into the rain. He couldn't stop her. Chibi had been hungry since the rain had started falling yesterday. Even without the rain, all she had to eat was nutritionless dried grass, and not much of it at that. He had to go out and look for something to eat.

She might catch cold—Kōji was worried about that. There is a cattle disease called infectious bovine rhinotracheitis, which has the same symptoms as the human cold. It can lead to pneumonia. This cow had been raised in a controlled climate—air conditioned in summer and heated in winter. If she was starting to suffer from malnutrition and then contracted pneumonia, it would be hard to save her.

He had neither antibiotics nor salt.

That's right, salt!

Suddenly it came to him. Cattle need salt. They need a small amount on a daily basis. He remembered taking care of Chibi when he was a boy. He always put some salt in her water. Chibi would noisily drink the entire bucket.

Sometimes he took Chibi to the sea. He let her swim. Her coat shone when he washed her with sea water. He also used dried seaweed with plenty of salt clinging to it in Chibi's bedding.

This was the secret to raising cattle on the island.

Kōji suddenly realized he hadn't given Chibi any salt since they'd fled the Matsuzaka Ranch.

Kōji roused himself from his stupor.

Chibi will die.

Suddenly he was afraid. He felt a sharp pain, as if an eagle's talon were lodged in his heart. He mustn't let her die. That thought rose to the surface of his mind. If she died here, he would have stolen her for nothing.

He had to go back down the mountain, he decided. He decided to act upon the thought that had surfaced and then faded from his mind again and again for the last several days. He would steal. If this kept on, he'd die of starvation before Chibi. He had to steal to survive. He'd steal some food and some salt.

Suddenly the sunken eyes in his thin face began to shine.

If they could just get through one winter, they'd be okay. In the spring, nutritious grass would sprout again. Flowers would bloom. All the greenery that would cover the mountain would be Chibi's food. He could start cultivating one of the deserted farm patches and grow food to feed himself.

He'd do whatever it took to survive. Whatever happened, he would see Chibi live out her natural life span.

That was the pledge he made to himself.

Kōji began to feel anxious about three hours later.

Chibi hadn't returned. He went to the entryway and called, but there was no response. The cold rain drenched the mountain.

Maybe she tripped and fell in the mud. Or maybe she started down into a valley and fell off a cliff.

His fear kept him frozen in place.

He could imagine Chibi driven by hunger, the cold rain pouring down on her bulk as she searched for food.

Kōji stepped out of the house. He didn't have an umbrella or a raincoat. He hadn't had the time to think of such things when he made his escape. He ran, the rain beating down on him. The path that he led Chibi through the forest every day was pretty much the same. He ran, calling Chibi's name.

But Chibi was nowhere to be found in their usual places.

Kōji returned to the deserted village. He was frozen to the bone. As he ran, the rain shrouded him so that he looked like a water sprite darting through the mist. The abandoned village was near a stream in a valley. He looked for Chibi up on the cliffs. He called out at the top of his lungs.

Chibi was nowhere to be found.

After running through the woods for about two hours, he still had neither seen nor heard any sign of Chibi. Dusk was approaching. Kōji returned to the abandoned house. He was shivering with cold. His lips were blue and twitching. His legs were shaky.

He undressed and wrung out his clothes.

Still naked, he climbed into his sleeping bag. He was shivering uncontrollably. Not only from cold, but from fear that Chibi was dead. Where had she gone in this freezing rain in search of food? Because she hadn't responded to Kōji's calls, maybe she had fallen down into a valley and died. Perhaps she'd broken a leg and was lying there helpless, too weak to cry out.

Whatever had happened, Chibi must be dead.

And even if she was safe, she would certainly catch pneumonia.

The sight of Chibi's thin back as she went out into the freezing rain to find something to eat was seared into Kōji's brain.

I want to die, thought Kōji. If Chibi dies, I can't go on living. What was the point of me rescuing her from Matsuzaka Ranch? After putting her through so much misery, I ended up causing her death just the same.

He felt something like a combination of remorse and misery, along with a rage that he didn't know where to direct. He gnashed his teeth.

The cold rain stopped the next morning.

Kōji awoke and looked around. Chibi wasn't there.

He lit a fire in the morning light and dried his clothes.

Before noon, he went out looking for Chibi again. He hadn't eaten for two days and his legs were weak and unsteady. He was exhausted. His stride was as halting as an old man's.

His suffering had also changed his face. Any trace of the freshness of youth was gone—he looked like an animal that had just recovered from an illness.

He searched for Chibi until late afternoon, then lifted his gaze, heavy with despair, up toward the mountain range.

His voice was hoarse. He was utterly drained. Sitting down in the grass, he stared up at the mountain tops with dull eyes lacking any spark of life. He was in a daze. His pupils merely reflected the surroundings, like a glass figurine.

He slumped over into sleep.

In his brief slumber, he had several dreams.

When he awakened again, the light was near the mountain peaks.

He dragged himself back to the abandoned village. He looked inside the house, and Chibi wasn't there. He hadn't expected her to be, but he felt as if his heart were being crushed.

He walked down the path through the forest.

It had occurred to him that Chibi might have descended to the town. The path, covered with weeds and fallen stones, led to the foot of the mountain. It was a single track. If you followed it down, you arrived in the town.

Maybe Chibi's instincts had taken her to town, where there would be food.

If that was the case, he had been abandoned.

Or perhaps maybe she was lying dead somewhere.

His knees shook as he descended the sloping path.

6

Kōji Tendō returned to the deserted village before noon on the following day.

He hid the food he'd stolen from a grocery store in Iitakachō—dried fish, rice, salt, sugar, and instant foods—in various places around the house where he was staying. He'd packed them in a box, and stolen a bicycle, too, which he used to carry his stash home.

He hid the bicycle along the way.

Chibi had not returned to the abandoned house. He was prepared for that. He intended to look for Chibi's body, making the food he'd stolen last as long as necessary. He'd keep looking until his stores ran out, and then if he still hadn't found Chibi, he'd leave the mountain.

He started searching in the afternoon.

It got dark very early that day.

The next day he went into the mountain woods from early morning.

He looked in places he'd never been before. Having eaten, he found that his strength had returned. He walked until about noon, but Chibi's voice was nowhere to be heard.

He lay down in a field of grass and rushes to sleep. He was tired from all the walking. He could sleep anywhere he could lie down.

He dreamed. It was a long dream. A very sad, meandering dream. He had no home. No family, no friends. He had no blanket, no food. Cold rain was falling. He was soaked, sleeping by the roadside. People were laughing. Why was he the only one in this pitiful state? Everyone else lived in fine houses.

A dark roaring wave rose around him. A frightening, threatening wave. The wave struck a boat. From the depths of the wave, he heard someone screaming.

Kōji struggled.

The boat slid into the wave's trough. His body flew up into the air. There was nothing to hold on to.

He screamed.

His scream woke him up. Something was pushing his back. He quickly rolled himself upright.

Chibi was standing in front of him.

"Chibi!" Kōji gasped.

Chibi let loose with a deep moo. She raised her muzzle to the sky and mooed again. Unable to speak, Kōji simply stared at Chibi. She was still thin. Yet thin as she was, her eyes sparkled as she looked back at Kōji. Something like morning dew glittered there.

Kōji sensed a wild strength in that light. This was something Chibi had never had before. It felt like...dignity.

Chibi knelt down and lowered herself to the ground. She began to chew her cud slowly. The moisture on her nose and lips glistened in the sunlight. Half-closing her eyes, she was lazily chewing her cud.

It was a behavior that suggested the sheer pleasure of having eaten her fill. The wrinkled skin hanging from her throat swayed slowly back and forth with the chewing motion.

Silently, Kōji sat there beside her.

There was no need to speak. There was nothing to say, nothing to ask. He was satisfied just to sit there watching Chibi chew her cud.

As he scratched her forehead, tears rose in his eyes.

Had she been delivered to the slaughterhouse, at this moment her meat would be on display in stores, her skin at the tanner's, her guts ripped out for organ meat.

She would never have experienced this restful moment, chewing her cud in the sunlight.

Kōji felt a powerful sense of relief. It was warmer than the sun's rays.

Kōji sat there stroking Chibi for a long time. Her odor had grown even stronger. That musty burnt smell rose from her warm, sun-splashed coat. It was the scent of pure wildness.

This was the third day since her departure into the freezing rain. Where had she gone? Kōji wondered. He'd worried she'd caught pneumonia in the cold and damp. He'd worried she'd broken a leg. Both of those worries were unfounded. Chibi had found something to eat somewhere, and eaten her fill. She'd probably sheltered from the rain under a tree. She'd probably slept under one at night. Kōji thought of her there, blacker than the night itself.

You're heartless, he whispered with his relieved smile.

Eventually Kōji stood up.

He decided to gather some dried grass and massage her. That was about the only thing he could do for her, given his circumstances. Massage is the best therapy for cattle. It helps their skin breathe and improves their circulation.

Kōji began to gather stiff dried grasses. As he did, he wondered whether Chibi had been looking for him, or whether she'd gone off looking for food and they'd just met by chance. He prayed it was the former. Cattle have a keen sense of smell. If she'd wanted to, she could find her way back to the abandoned house. On the way back, she'd have picked up Kōji's scent.

That's what he wanted to believe.

He heard something behind him. It must be Chibi, he thought. Kōji, who had been crouching, stood up. There was a rustling in the rushes ahead of him. Something was rushing straight at him.

At first he thought it was a dog. In the next moment, he realized what it was. A wild boar. The dark form of a wild boar was rushing at him through the grass. The thick mane of hair on its powerful shoulders was standing straight up.

He could see its white tusks. The grass stems parted to either side as they were struck by the tusks.

Kōji felt faint. Clearly the boar was heading for him. He could hear it snapping its tusks aggressively.

Kōji looked for a place to escape. There was no refuge in sight. If there had been a tree, he could have shinnied up it, but he was in the middle of a field of rushes. He emitted a short scream. The boar was upon him. He leaped sideways to avoid it. The boar circled and came at Kōji again. He heard the sound of the animal's snapping tusks at his back.

A wild boar's tusks are razor sharp. He had heard that they could sever a leg.

He thought the end was upon him.

He ran as fast as he could.

Suddenly something appeared to his side. Something huge and black. It emitted a ferocious cry. It took a moment before he realized it was Chibi.

Kōji stopped. He looked behind him. His blood froze.

Chibi was bellowing angrily. A thick "moooo" split the air. With her head brushing against the ground, she was charging the boar. She held her horns out before her. Her tail was extended in a straight line, parallel with the ground. Clumps of earth dug up by her hooves flew through the air.

The boar stopped.

Chibi hit the boar with her mighty form. Her four legs were powerful. Her horns rose up into the air. Her thick neck flew up in an arc. Kōji thought the boar had been tossed into the air, but he seemed to have sidestepped the cow's attack.

"Chibi!" screamed Kōji.

Chibi's four legs were firmly anchored in an attack stance. Her head remained down, her horns aimed at the boar.

The boar stood several meters in front of her, gnashing its tusks. Only then did Kōji notice its bloody shoulder.

"The boar's wounded! Run, Chibi!" he shrieked. A wounded boar is madness incarnate. It's fearless. Chibi would be slashed to bits.

The boar kicked up earth. Chibi bellowed. As she bellowed, she pawed the ground with her front hooves. The boar rushed directly at her. Chibi kicked at the earth and launched forward. Two masses, one huge and black, the other a bundle of pure rage, collided in the grass.

Chibi tossed the boar upwards with her horns. The boar regained its footing and gnashed its tusks. Clumps of earth went flying.

Chibi bellowed.

The boar rushed at Chibi like a lance.

Just seconds before, Kōji noticed something like an arrow dashing through the grass toward them. It was white and was approaching at an astonishing speed.

The white object struck the boar that was attacking Chibi.

It was a white dog. The dog bit into the boar's rear leg. He saw a cloud of dust, and the boar spun around. The dog leaped out of the boar's way. The boar faced the dog and attacked. The dog spun around and avoided the boar's tusks.

The boar turned to face Chibi again.

The dog let out a short angry yelp. It bit into the boar's haunch again. The boar spun around. The dog leaped away. They were obscured by a cloud of dust.

Kōji had no idea how long this fight to the death went on.

Suddenly an old man rushed into the field.

A gunshot went off.

Startled, Chibi began to run across the field.

Kōji chased after her.

7

The sun had set.

Eikichi Mukōda and Kōji Tendō sat facing each other across the open hearth.

They were in an abandoned village one village beyond the one where Kōji had been staying. The house belonged to Mukōda, a hunter. He lived there alone, but not throughout the whole year. He only stayed there during the hunting season.

Mukōda had supported himself as a hunter since he was young. His son was head of the family now, and they lived in Matsuzaka.

"What, you don't eat meat?"

Boar meat simmered in the pot. Kōji had only been eating the vegetables.

"Since the cow I kept as a boy was sold, I haven't been able to eat meat."

"Ah."

Mukōda poured some *shōchū* into a bowl. He was slowly sipping the *shōchū* and eating boar meat. He didn't know what to say in response to Kōji's admission.

Seeing the boy and the cow, he had pretty much figured it out.

He brought them back to his house. The cow was in the barn. He lived here about half the year, so the house was well kept. The others in the village were falling apart, but his was in good repair.

So you're the Kōji Tendō who stole the cow from Matsuzaka Ranch, he said. Kōji was silent. I don't intend to tell anyone, said Mukōda. Reassured, Kōji nodded.

He began to explain haltingly. About Chibi whom he'd raised as a boy. About starting to work at Matsuzaka Ranch and meeting Kikunogo, which seemed like a reunion.

Mukōda listened silently.

The police investigation of the theft of Kikunogo was over and done with, since the Matsuzaka Ranch had withdrawn its complaint and announced that it gave Kikunogo to the boy. The public, however, viewed the ranch's action with skepticism. They assumed that the boy must be in possession of the secrets of fattening Matsuzaka beef cows or some other information that would damage the Matsuzaka brand.

Mukōda had no interest in the matter. The Matsuzaka methods of fattening cows were, he thought, inhumane. But he didn't eat

Matsuzaka beef, and the world was full of inhumane things. Now in his mid-sixties, Mukōda had little interest in the world any more.

But listening to Kōji Tendō's explanation, he couldn't help but feel a sense of wonderment. Kōji said he couldn't bear the thought of Kikunogo being killed. That was his sole motive.

It wasn't a protest against dosing beef cattle with antibiotics, as the public suspected, nor against the working conditions on the ranch. Even if the ranch had been flaunting the ban on antibiotics, they would have been putting them in the water or feed, so the boy would have no way of knowing about it. He didn't have access to any secrets.

Matsuzaka Ranch must have dropped the charges, then, because they were afraid the mass media would start writing stories about the fattening methods they employed, and the negative publicity would damage their brand. Six million yen was a cheap price to pay for avoiding the unwanted public scrutiny.

Mukōda understood that. These were the days when Japanese fishermen had become the target of an international outcry for their slaughter of dolphins, which they said interfered with their catches. It was easy to assume that the fattening methods used to produce Matsuzaka beef could just as easily become the fresh outrage of the day. And then the reputation of that marbled meat—soft as butter, produced by pouring unlimited quantities of rich feed, alcohol, and a battery of pharmaceuticals into these factory beasts, cows in name only—might take a serious hit.

No, Mukōda felt wonderment for another reason.

The perfect simplicity of Kōji Tendō's motive.

Nothing is more powerful than a simple motive—Kōji's utter determination to prevent Kikunogo from being killed.

There was nothing he could say to the boy.

"So what are you going to do?"

That was the question—how Kōji Tendō was going to survive. He wasn't accused of theft any longer, so he could go back to Matsuzaka. If he returned the cow, the ranch wouldn't pursue the matter. He could start a new life.

It was impossible for a boy without any money or skills to survive on his own with a cow in the mountains. He must be aware of that from the two weeks or so he'd spent in hiding.

Kōji answered in a low voice: "I'll wait until spring. In spring, there'll be grass."

"What are you going to do when it snows?"

Kōji remained silent.

"If you had a supply of hay put aside, you might get by. But with nothing, the cow will starve to death. And not just the cow. What about you? To survive, a person needs a house to live in, food, clothing, wood to keep warm. And a lot of other things. You have to work to get those things."

Kōji didn't reply.

Silently, he laid his chopsticks aside and looked down.

The wind could be heard blowing across the river.

"I've been a hunter for a long time. I don't know how to do anything else. There've always been a lot of wild boars in the area. When I was young, it was fun shooting things. Now, though, there's nothing fun about it. Mostly I hate killing. I'd quit if I could. But my family in Matsuzaka City, they're just scraping by. The boars I kill, it helps out."

To be honest, Mukōda didn't like hunting boars. He'd felt that way for years. He wanted to quit. Boars have children and parents, too, after all. But he couldn't be a burden on his son. Though he looked on his skill at killing animals as a sad fate, he couldn't quit.

But seeing the boy leaving the boar's meat untouched and looking down gloomily at the floor, he realized nothing he could say would make any difference.

When he decided to run off with Kikunogo, the boy must have been prepared for the consequences. At eighteen, one grasps the consequences of one's actions, at least to some extent. This boy had thrown caution to the wind. He had tossed it aside and willingly entered a world of darkness.

"Anyway." Mukōda poured himself some more *shōchū*. Wind blowing through cracks in the house made the lamp's flame shimmy.

"You can stay here as long as you like. I owe something to your cow, too."

If it hadn't been for the cow, Mukōda would have been in big trouble. He had hit the boar but failed to kill it. A wounded wild boar can go insane with the pain.

The boar had attacked the boy in an open field, meaning he had no way to escape. He could never outrun the boar. He would have been seriously wounded or killed. The thought sent chills down Mukōda's spine.

He was pitiful.

Kikunogo had saved the situation. Some cows are meek, others are fearless. Some run away when they see a dog, some chase after it. But this was a wild boar. Mukōda had never heard of a cow charging a wild boar.

Mukōda didn't know whether the cow had bellowed and attacked the boar because she was trying to rescue the boy or not. Maybe she was just a fearless cow. That was probably the better explanation.

But the fact was that she did rescue the boy. She also rescued Mukōda. The boy believed that Kikunogo, whom he had rescued, had now rescued him. He could imagine how this must have strengthened the connection the boy felt to the animal.

Maybe, he thought, the boy's decision to save the cow from the slaughterhouse had been the right one after all.

Even if he couldn't say if it was right or not, having purged herself of the marbled fat that the Matsuzaka ranchers had forced on her and that the Japanese public so enjoyed, Kikunogo had been sufficiently restored to her wild state to fend off a wounded wild boar, and she and the boy were tightly bound to each other.

Mukōda slowly shook his head.

There are things in the world for which there just aren't easy answers, he thought.

If he told Kōji to return the cow to the Matsuzaka Ranch and start a new life, the boy might commit suicide with the animal.

But it would be nearly impossible for them to survive the winter in these present circumstances. Even if he got through the winter and lasted until spring, the future was equally grim. Someday he'd have to get rid of Kikunogo and start a new life. That was the fate of human beings.

The insensitivity of the boy's father, abruptly selling the cow the boy had raised to the slaughterhouse, was deplorable; his mother's irresponsibility, rolling around naked in the woods with a village youth, was infuriating.

Kōji Tendō's parents were the ones responsible for making him a young man of such a dark and intransigent character.

8

December 15.

Unusually, snow fell on the Sekiryō Mountains on the border between Mie and Nara prefectures before the year was out.

For some time they'd been predicting it would be an especially cold winter.

Senji Nakamichi, posted to the local police box, had been at the Matsuzaka Police Station since morning. The police chief had a special message for his officers concerning the holiday season. He asked everyone to be on the alert, since lately there had been a rise in crime.

There was a chart showing recent crimes in Mie Prefecture.

While glancing casually at the chart, Nakamichi's eyes were drawn to one particular spot. This month there were three thefts in Iitakachō in adjacent Iinan County. Two were thefts of food, and the third from a store that sold farming supplies. The farm supply store reported a theft of 140,000 yen. The thefts from the food stores were much smaller; each of them reported thefts of goods totaling less than thirty thousand yen.

Food.

Nakamichi remembered the map of the area around Iitakachō. It was a small level area surrounded by mountains on both sides. National Highway 166 crossed the Daikō Mountains and went on to Nara Prefecture. On the right were the Takami Highlands. On the left was another mountainous area. Over the mountains was Ōdaichō.

The truck that had been used to cart Kikunogo away had been abandoned on the outskirts of Ōdaichō.

"That was it. Ah, now I see," murmured Nakamichi to himself. He left the station.

Three days later he took a day off.

He left his house on a motorbike and drove toward Iitakachō.

He had discovered that there were several abandoned villages in the Takami Highlands. He was sure that Kōji Tendō was hiding out in one of them. Kōji Tendō had purposely abandoned the truck on the other side of the mountains that had been his destination.

Very clever.

But Nakamichi wasn't angry. If anything, he was worried. The police had closed the book on the theft of Kikunogo. It looked like Matsuzaka Ranch had given up their private investigation, too. They were far too busy right now. They were completely occupied with preparations for getting their choice Matsuzaka beef ready for sale for the holidays.

At the end of the year, lines formed to purchase the highest quality beef at three thousand yen per hundred grams, to send as presents to important clients and customers.

With the bustle of the approaching holiday season, everyone had forgotten about Kikunogo.

It seemed that the Matsuzaka Ranch had succeeded in protecting their brand.

No one had been hurt.

That's what Nakamichi believed. He was glad the whole thing had been settled peacefully.

But now Kōji Tendō had started stealing. In all likelihood, this was his doing. Nakamichi had been afraid this would happen. Theft was really the only way he could survive with Kikunogo, off in the mountain recesses.

Though superficially it seemed that the Kikunogo incident had ended without hurting anyone, actually there were some who had been seriously harmed. Kōji Tendō and Kikunogo. Nakamichi had a very grim feeling when he thought of the boy and the cow hiding away in the snowy Takami Highlands, stealing to survive.

Clearly, this would end very badly, unless something was done.

The Matsuzaka Ranch continued to prosper, while the boy and Kikunogo were on their way to imminent self-destruction. Whereas the boy must have had special feelings for Kikunogo that made him steal the cow, he must also have been protesting the way Matsuzaka cattle were raised and marketed.

Nakamichi had a very strong desire to somehow prevent cornering the boy into a miserable defeat.

There was no trace of the boy or the cow in the first deserted village. It had been abandoned several years ago, and stood in silent obscurity against the backdrop of winter. Once people depart, their artifacts quickly decay. It seemed a symbol of the fragility and transience of human existence.

The narrow road had half-returned to wild fields. At times he had to get off the motorbike and push it as he climbed. The first cold blasts of winter whined in the woods on either side.

Nakamichi arrived at the next deserted village after noon.

He walked through it, looking into each decaying house.

In the last house, on the outskirts of the village, he found traces of the boy and the cow. There was cow manure in the yard. There were signs of a cooking fire. Nakamichi examined the scene carefully. He noticed that these signs were old.

So he's moved on.

He looked out of the house with bewilderment. There were patches of snow here and there on the ground. It had been frozen by the icy winds.

There were two more deserted villages in the area. By the time he visited them both, it would be dark. What should he do, he wondered.

In the end, he got back on the motorbike. If he returned empty handed after having found traces of his quarry, the entire trip would have been wasted. There was no reason he couldn't ride down the mountain in the dark, if it came to that.

He headed toward the peak.

There were no traces in the next deserted village.

Nakamichi got on the motorbike again. He had to climb a fairly high peak to reach the next deserted village. Toward the top there was a lot of snow. There were no villages beyond the last deserted site. There were no roads.

He was sure the boy and the cow were hiding there. There was no place else to go. He felt he understood the boy's thinking: having gone down to the town to steal supplies, he was frightened, and took refuge as far away as possible.

It was a difficult ride, but he made it over the snowy peak.

He could see the last village from the peak. In the distance a valley stream flowed. There were a dozen or so houses scattered near the stream.

Smoke was rising from one of them.

Pushing the motorbike, Nakamichi began to descend. He was afraid the sound of the motor would scare the boy off.

He hid the bike before entering the village.

He approached the house with the smoke rising from it.

A dog and an old man were sitting around the hearth. Seeing them there, his heart sunk.

"Who are you?"

Eikichi Mukōda spoke first. The sudden appearance of a stranger in his house startled him.

"My name is Senji Nakamichi. I'm from the Matsuzaka Police Station. May I come in?"

"Sure."

I've been expecting this, thought Mukōda.

Nakamichi sat near the hearth.

"I've come here looking for a boy and a cow."

"That would be Kōji Tendō and Kikunogo."

Pouring some tea, Mukōda looked at Nakamichi. When the visitor said he'd come from the Matsuzaka Police Station, at first Mukōda thought he must be a detective, but he didn't look right. He was short and nondescript. Moreover, he was too old.

"So he's here…"

"He's out in the woods with the cow."

"I see." Nakamichi felt a slight sense of relief.

"Are you going to bring them back?"

"That's my intent."

"I see," said Mukōda, nodding and then falling silent.

Sipping his tea, Nakamichi looked at Mukōda. His face was brown and deeply etched with wrinkles. With his head down, he looked angry.

"Kōji Tendō is suspected of some thefts down in Iitakachō."

"I know."

"You know about it?"

"I had a feeling he'd stolen some things, but there was nothing I could do about it. I can't tell him to kill the cow. But you can. That's your duty."

Nakamichi said nothing.

"You'll arrest him on charges of theft, and while you're holding him you'll return the cow to the Matsuzaka ranch. I knew from the beginning that's how it would end."

That might be best for the boy anyway, thought Mukōda. Thievery was the only way Kōji Tendō could manage to stay alive. Sooner or later, it would come to a bad end. The cow was too big. It was wrong for him to love the cow. There was something in Kōji Tendō's emotional nature that had remained unchanged, stopped in time, from his boyhood. He refused to recognize that good doesn't always prevail in our world—that's not the way it works. He couldn't go on this way forever.

Breaking out of his cocoon and moving forward would be extremely painful. It wasn't something he could do on his own. He needed to have that cocoon ripped open by the police—he needed to be forced to grow up.

"How's Kikunogo?"

"Unrecognizable." Mukōda shook his head. The animal was no longer a Matsuzaka cow. The flab that had been forced on her frame in Matsuzaka had completely disappeared.

"Have you ever heard the legend of the cow demon?" asked Mukōda, looking down at his tea cup.

Nakamichi had. In Kyushu the cow demon was supposed to be a sea creature, with the body of a crab or a spider and the head of a cow. But in these mountain areas, an older legend existed, that of a massive beast in the form of a cow. Ancient stories told of warriors battling the creature, and not always winning.

"Well, imagine an emaciated cow demon." He almost whispered.

Mukōda told Nakamichi about his initial encounter with Kōji Tendō and Kikunogo, how she'd regained a wildness that had made her strong enough to take on an injured wild boar.

"An emaciated cow demon," murmured Nakamichi.

Silence fell.

The lid on the kettle hanging on a hook over the hearth rattled softly.

The voice of a cow could be heard in the distance, blending with the cold wind.

The dog rose softly and went out to greet them.

Mukōda and Nakamichi remained silent.

After a time, they could hear the cow being put in the barn.

Kōji Tendō stepped into the earthen-floored entryway.

Kōji saw Nakamichi and stopped short. He knew immediately that Nakamichi had come after him.

He turned on his heel.

"Wait!" called Nakamichi to the boy's back. Kōji Tendō, who had been about to dash off, stopped.

"I'm a cop in a police box near the Matsuzaka Ranch. My name is Senji Nakamichi. Even at my age, I'm still just a beat cop in a police box. You don't need to be afraid of me. Will you come here a minute?"

Kōji turned around. Nakamichi smiled.

Without speaking, Kōji sat next to the rear of the hearth.

"I'm sure you heard from Mr. Mukōda, but Matsuzaka Ranch has given you Kikunogo. The police aren't looking for you."

Nakamichi looked at the thin boy. He was slight. There was no sign of the youthfulness you'd expect in a boy of eighteen. His skin was lifeless, perhaps from malnutrition.

"I didn't come here to arrest you. I came to bring you back. You're going to die here in these mountains. I know you love Kikunogo. But cows live a long time. By the time she's lived out her life, what do you think will have become of you?"

Kōji Tendō was silent.

"For example, even if you're able to grow food and support yourself, you'll end up completely alone and out of place in the world. What will you do then?"

Still no word from the boy.

"And you've been stealing things in Iitakachō, haven't you?"

Kōji Tendō still didn't reply.

Mukōda was silent, too. An expression of deep despair clouded the boy's face. Mukōda avoided the boy's gaze, looking down in adamant silence.

"What do you think will happen to Kikunogo if you end up getting caught the next time you steal something?"

Kōji Tendō remained silent.

"I have nothing to do with what's going on in Iitakachō. Let's just forget about the thefts. Won't you come back with me? You can return the cow to Matsuzaka Ranch. I'll find you a job."

This was the purpose of Nakamichi's visit.

Mukōda had told him the boy's motive for stealing the cow. It was a simple motive. Because it was so simple, he could see what the boy was thinking as clear as day. At first everyone had assumed the theft was a protest against the cruelty of the fattening methods employed by Matsuzaka Ranch. What other reason could there have been?

Even after the Matsuzaka Ranch dropped the charges of theft and gave Kikunogo to the boy, that doubt remained in the public's mind, because otherwise Matsuzaka Ranch's actions didn't make sense. Unless they had something to hide, why should they roll over like that?

The police had given up their investigation, but this turn of events only intensified Nakamichi's interest in the boy. He wanted to understand his motive. He hoped for at least a glimpse of the state of mind that had impelled him to steal the cow.

Part of Nakamichi's interest were his own criticisms of Matsuzaka beef. He'd never have a chance to eat something so expensive. Nor did he want to. He believed there was something perverse in raising cows that way. He hadn't thought about it deeply, but he felt that there was something profoundly wrong with people who so prized the richly marbled meat of Matsuzaka cows, produced in such an inhumane fashion—something like the primal sinfulness of uncontrolled appetite.

Yes, there was something evil about it. To be so driven by one's appetites was ghoulish, he felt. He remembered reading a story somewhere about a high-ranking monk who was so fond of wild yams that his nose grew as long as a yam and itched constantly, like grated yams do on the skin. It was unnatural to allow oneself to become be so obsessed with anything.

The stomach lining of Matsuzaka cows isn't suitable for eating they say. It's so stretched out from being stuffed with feed that it's too thin to grill.

The time had come for someone to speak out against this, Nakamichi thought vaguely.

But the quiet Kōji Tendō, who had stolen Kikunogo, said nothing.

He must have something he wants to say.

If he was driven to self-destruction, the bud representing the possibility of a productive adult life that had formed in those three years of working at the Matsuzaka Ranch would be snipped off. Even if he never said anything about the beef-production methods at the ranch, Nakamichi wanted Kōji Tendō to share with him, at least, what was in his mind.

The boy remained downcast.

"How about it?" asked Nakamichi after a while,

"Let me think about it," said Kōji, bowing slightly. Then he stood.

Nakamichi and Mukōda both knew that Kōji was going to the barn. They heard the barn door opening against the background of the wind.

They heard the footsteps of the cow.

Nakamichi and Mukōda looked at each other. Neither said anything. They listened silently as the sound of the footsteps trailed off. Soon all that remained was the wailing of the wind.

Mukōda brought the *shōchū*. Without speaking, he poured some into Nakamichi's teacup.

Mukōda knew that Kōji Tendō would reject Nakamichi's offer. This was a boy who, no matter how hungry he was, refused to put even one piece of boar flesh in his mouth.

If he returned Kikunogo, she'd be fattened up again at the Matsuzaka Ranch. When a heifer reached the age of four, her fat became tinged with yellow. No one would buy it unless it was white. Kikunogo could still be fattened up for slaughter.

Given a constant supply of enriched feed, antibiotics, and drugs. Made to drink beer, and massaged with *shōchū*. Fed sweet saké and brown sugar.

Her cow scent would disappear and the lost weight would return.

She'd be sent to the slaughterhouse.

He knew the boy couldn't endure that.

The boy could not condemn the cow to death.

Kikunogo had saved his life from a wounded boar.

Mukōda poured more *shōchū*.

The cold winds swept over the house.

The dog, who seemed to have followed Kōji halfway, returned.

Mukōda downed the *shōchū* and stepped out of the house.

He could see the mountain peak from the yard. It was covered with old snow. The boy and the cow were ascending the peak. One large black dot and one small black dot, both slowly moving upward.

Nakamichi stood beside him.

"Emaciated cow demon," Nakamichi thought to himself.

He thought of the wind blowing against the chest of the boy, leading the thin cow up to the snowy peak.

"What's beyond that peak?" he asked Mukōda in a hoarse voice.

"Nothing."

Mukōda slowly shook his head. There was nothing back there. Nowhere for the boy and the cow to go.

The cold wind whipped through the night.

The Mysterious Sea Creature

Naméso: A mysterious sea creature feared by fishermen in the Inland Sea. Thought to be a kind of shark; legend has it that if a *naméso* overtakes a boat, the boat will sink unless the creature is speared.

—*Kōjien* dictionary

1

"Old man." Drinking her miso soup, Ishi looked at Jūkichi sharply. "Why aren't you catching any fish?"

"What do you mean, 'Why?'" asked Jūkichi, shrugging. Actually, he wasn't so much shrugging as he just had a short neck. He was short, too. And his back was hunched. His bent spine showed his age.

"It's funny."

Jūkichi placed a piece of stonefish from the soup in his mouth. His head remained down. He made no effort to meet Ishi's glare.

"The fish aren't biting," he mumbled.

"For ten days?" Her tone suddenly changed. "Are you saying that not one fish has bitten for ten days?"

Silence.

"Are you hiding something?"

"No," said Jūkichi, shaking his head.

"Are you going senile on me?" asked Ishi sarcastically.

Jūkichi put his chopsticks down. Without looking at Ishi, he took his lunch and left the house.

Ishi watched with irritation as Jūkichi's curved back disappeared in the morning mist.

This was the tenth day since Jūkichi had stopped catching fish. He hadn't brought home a single fish in ten days.

The fish hadn't stopped biting. Ishi knew that was just an excuse. Jūkichi was famous for his fishing expertise. Of course there were times when, whether fishing with a line or a net, you had a string of bad luck. But this had never happened to Jūkichi. Jūkichi could read the sea. He looked at its color, at the shape of the waves, at the changes in the currents. At a glance, he knew what kind of fish were where, and whether they were biting or not.

The day that Jūkichi stopped catching fish would be the day the sea died.

He's hiding something, Ishi thought. She looked blankly up at the sky.

She didn't know what he was hiding. Not a woman, of course. Jūkichi was eighty years old. Even if he'd been forty, no woman would have him. He was plug-ugly, clumsy, and rarely spoke. His honest nature was his only virtue.

It couldn't be gambling. Ishi would have been glad if he'd had the smarts for gambling.

She had checked with the fisherman's cooperative. She thought that maybe he'd been selling his catch secretly.

She was wrong.

Jūkichi bought live bait every day. But he hadn't caught anything.

"That senile old fart," Ishi silently cursed him.

She cursed him, but she was afraid. Jūkichi's catch was their only means of support. If he couldn't catch any more fish, they'd have nothing to live on. They had no savings to speak of, and only a little vegetable plot.

Even on their island, Jūkichi was the poorest of the poor.

It was all because of his thick headedness.

He had no talent with machines. When he was young, he broke his arm once when trying to start a boat's motor. It was an engine you start by turning a crank. Ever since then, he was afraid to touch an engine.

Engines today didn't even have cranks any more. You just pushed the starter button. But Jūkichi stubbornly refused to use an engine.

He went out to sea in a little boat that he rowed with a single scull at the back.

The distance he could travel out to sea by sculling was limited. That's why he became an expert at reading the currents. As he sculled, he carefully read the extremely complex currents of the Inland Sea. He rode the currents both going out to fish and coming back to the harbor. Jūkichi couldn't be a fisherman if he ignored the currents.

Of course he also read the wind. The wind could power his boat even if he was traveling against the current.

For Jūkichi, sculling wasn't as difficult as most people thought.

He read the currents and the wind, so he knew the sea very well. Fishermen who can go wherever they like with the horsepower of an engine attached to their boats, without concerning themselves with currents or wind, don't even try to understand the sea. All they're thinking about is hauling every fish in the sea up in their nets.

Jūkichi also hated nets.

With his talent for fishing, if he'd used a net, by now Jūkichi would be living in a palace and sitting on a pile of money. The same would probably have been true if he'd used an engine.

The Inland Sea was polluted. The fishing industry was in an inescapable decline, they said. It was true that it wasn't as prosperous as it had been right before and after the war. But again, it depended on the place. The fishing was good off of Jūkichi's island. The size of the catches had fallen, but the price of fish had risen. The fish caught around the island didn't end up in the mouths of ordinary people. They were tasty, so they were bought up by high-class restaurants.

People who were still fishing were all, without exception, well off now.

Except, of course, for Jūkichi.

Only Jūkichi was poor. But it was a pure-hearted poverty.

Jūkichi never harmed the fish he caught. He took care to catch them cleanly and quickly. It was said that a fish caught by Jūkichi wouldn't be missing so much as a single scale. He was always able to sell his fish for just a little bit more than anyone else.

People used to call him "Master Jūkichi" behind his back. They used "master" teasingly, but also with a degree of respect.

Now Jūkichi hadn't caught a fish in ten days.

There was fear in Ishi's eyes.

If he wasn't hiding anything, it meant he was getting senile.

2

Jūkichi stopped the boat in the muddy shallows.

The height of summer was past. You could see that in the color of the waves. The passing of the seasons is apparent in the sea before it shows in the vegetation on land. Everything was clearly visible on the waters.

A reed blind stretched over the boat as a sun shade. Through it, the sun cast a striped pattern on the boat's seat.

A gentle breeze caressed his skin.

Jūkichi had caught fifty horse mackerel.

Fishermen who used a pole never caught horse mackerel to sell at the market. They only caught them to eat themselves. But recently Jūkichi was only catching horse mackerel.

He took the scull again.

Riding a current, he went out farther.

Damn Ishi. His wife's angry visage flashed across his mind. *What a worthless old hag*, he thought. *Such a big mouth.* All she did was walk around all day flapping her jaws. If he didn't catch something today, there'd be trouble. It wasn't that he was afraid of Ishi, but the thought of having to listen to her curses and her ranting was more than he could bear.

He decided to catch a butterfish. Along with red sea bream and Spanish mackerel, it was one of the most expensive fish that you could catch in the Inland Sea. If he wanted to, he could easily earn ten or twenty thousand yen with his catch.

When he reached a spot midway out, he dropped a line.

The sea was a rich, golden color. The line went into the water at an angle and was soon tight. This was the moment that Jūkichi felt most alive. He thought of the massive bulk of the sea. He imagined a bottomless ocean as springy and glutinous as jelly.

It was an unknown realm for Jūkichi, too. The fishing line was transmitting the feeling of that unknown realm to him. And his eighty years of life were in that feeling.

His whole life, Jūkichi had lived in the sea. All he knew was the sea. When he was younger, he wanted to know other things. He imagined love, he imagined the big city, he imagined many things. All the symbols of the things he desired in life were in the sea.

He no longer had any desires, but in the depths of the massive sea there was the illusion of a shining city. He felt as if all the dreams a man could have were there in the sea.

Something hit his line hard.

Jūkichi smoothly let the line out. The neatly coiled line leaped over the thick bamboo gunwale of the boat.

Jūkichi manipulated the scull with his left hand. From the way the line was going out, it wasn't a butterfish. It was something really big.

After about thirty fathoms, the line stopped.

Holding the line, he could feel the fish's intentions in his fingertips. The fish was wondering what to do. It was looking up and wondering how skilled the person on the other end of the line was.

It's a Spanish mackerel, thought Jūkichi. They came to the Inland Sea in May and June to spawn. That's when they were at their best. They didn't taste as good after they'd spawned. Then from autumn through winter, their flavor improved again. Right now, their flavor was neither good nor bad.

The fish started to move again.

While operating the scull with his left hand, Jūkichi sent the boat forward, together with the fish. He made the boat match the fish's speed. The fish was swimming heroically.

"Go, go, swim as fast as you like," murmured Jūkichi. These days, Jūkichi often imagined the eyes of the fish. He imagined its eyes as it tried its best to escape. He had gradually stopped enjoying the touch of the line. He started to feel an aversion to taking a life. The feeling was very strong, and getting stronger every day.

The fish held out for close to an hour.

Jūkichi wiped the perspiration from his forehead with the back of his hand.

He was tired. *I'm old*, he thought. *I know I get older every year. It must be a huge fish, but it's pitiful that it's wearing me out like this.*

A red-throated loon was next to Jūkichi, looking at him with its ruby eyes.

It was ten days ago that he'd seen the loon.

Red-throated loons are beautiful migratory birds. They're excellent divers, and fishermen regard them as good luck, because they show them where the fish are.

That day Jūkichi was off the east coast of Iwanejima, waiting for the current. Iwanejima was an uninhabited island about two kilometers in circumference. It was covered by a forest of stunted pines. The only beach was on the island's east coast. The green of the pines cast a shadow on the pure white sand.

Since boats with engines didn't need to wait for the currents, no one came near the island any more.

A single loon was floating in the sea off the beach. Since the Inland Sea had become polluted, loons rarely came there any more.

When Jūkichi approached the island in his boat, the loon took off, leaving a white wake on the ocean surface. It looked at Jūkichi as it flew off. Its glossy eyes were red as blood. Jūkichi watched it fly off, thinking that he'd seen a bad omen.

When Jūkichi lowered his gaze to the beach again, he gasped.

A jet black monster lay in the water off the shore.

"A *naméso*," said Jūkichi softly.

It was a beast known by the fishermen as a *naméso*. He didn't know its scientific name. Now it would be called a dolphin or a finless porpoise.

Others say it's a kind of shark, a monster fish that only lives in the Inland Sea.

Not much is known about it.

It was said to school, and before the Inland Sea became polluted, large herds of them used to be found there. They were the fisherman's most dreaded foe. They chased the fish away. They ate fish that had been netted. They were the thugs of the fishing grounds.

Jūkichi hadn't seen a *naméso* in a long time.

This one was trying to beach itself.

Jūkichi grabbed a gaff. It was an instinctive move. Here was the fisherman's detested enemy, after all.

The *naméso* didn't move. Jūkichi put down the gaff. Looking closely, he saw a gash on its back. The skin around it was waving back and forth in the waves. The *naméso* seemed to be panting in pain.

At first Jūkichi thought that the greedy loon had done this.

Jūkichi looked vacantly at the *naméso*. Every once in a while it would lift its head out of the water. It was breathing in painful gulps.

This was the first time Jūkichi had gotten a full look at a *naméso*. Not just Jūkichi, but most fishermen. It was a mysterious fish, which is why its proper scientific name was still unknown. They were hardly ever caught. Once there was a big hubbub about the foot of a human child being found in the stomach of a *naméso* that was put up for sale in the Takamatsu City fish market.

From that time on it was believed to be a fearsome creature that ate not only other fish but people, too. There was also a legend that if a *naméso* overtakes a boat, the boat will sink.

Jūkichi got out of his boat and approached the *naméso* cautiously. He held an axe in his hand, in case the beast suddenly attacked.

When he was about a meter away, he stopped. The *naméso* lifted its head. It cried out, *Kyuu, kyuu,* two or three times as if in pain, shaking its round head.

Jūkichi jumped back in surprise. He hadn't expected the *naméso* to make a sound. With the axe still in hand, he looked at it. The head was round. It looked like it was wearing a hat. Its mouth projected slightly. Its eyes were small and round. It was looking directly at Jūkichi.

It wore an extremely pitiful expression. As he looked at the *naméso*, Jūkichi realized that the penetrating sound the animal had made just now was an expression of sadness. "So that's it," he murmured. Jūkichi lowered the axe. Sweat was running down his forehead.

"You want me to help you?" asked Jūkichi, thinking at the same time how idiotic the idea was.

A *naméso* wouldn't ask a human being, much less a fisherman, for help. And he thought it was very strange that a fisherman would even consider offering.

Jūkichi squatted at the water's edge. The perspiration still dripping from his forehead, he looked at the *naméso*.

The *naméso* shook its head once more and cried out again.

He could see a row of small teeth. He'd expected the animal to have sharp teeth like an orca or crocodile, but he was puzzled when he saw that they were small and cute, like a baby's.

The *naméso* was appealing to Jūkichi. It was trying its best to tell him something.

Should I help it? Jūkichi asked himself. The *naméso* was still the fisherman's rival it'd always been. The two couldn't peacefully coexist. But with the *naméso* right there before his eyes, Jūkichi couldn't hate it. For the life of him, he didn't know why.

It seemed to him a sin to abandon the animal.

He walked up to it. Very cautiously, he touched it. The *naméso* remained still. He looked at the wound. The skin was broken, and transparent fluid was oozing from it. It wasn't a very deep cut. It looked as if it had gotten caught in some kind of net and had struggled desperately to escape. Perhaps its gasping was a sign of that exertion rather than pain from the wound.

He had no medicine to treat it. There was some iodine on the boat. The wound was underwater, so to apply any medicine, he'd have to pull the animal up on to the beach.

Jūkichi stood there in the water, at a loss for what to do.

Eventually, he walked up on the beach.

"Wait there," he said to the *naméso*, walking into the pines. He knew that mugwort grew there. He found some and brought it back. He climbed into his boat, put the mugwort in an empty can, and crushed it. When it was a thick, liquid consistency, he mixed some iodine in with it.

Jūkichi had no idea whether this mixture of mugwort and iodine would be effective. He peered at the strange potion and chuckled to himself.

Stripping down to his loincloth, he went back in the water. He walked up to his waist and pushed the *naméso*'s body. As he did so, he wondered at what he was doing. If anyone had seen him, they'd think he was insane. The *naméso* remained still, but Jūkichi couldn't know whether it was aggressive. Maybe it was all just a trap, so it could devour Jūkichi.

He kept pushing, as he thought about this. The animal was very large. Its girth was bigger than Jūkichi's arm span. And it was heavy, its skin slippery. He moved it a little at a time. He was prepared for it to suddenly attack, but there was no sign of that.

Grunting as he pushed, Jūkichi managed to get the animal up on the beach.

He brought the can. He soaked a towel in the liquid and squeezed the juice over the wound. He carefully applied it to the entire cut. He closed the cut flaps of skin and pressed the wound with the towel.

The *naméso* remained still through all of this.

The harsh light of the sun struck the wound. The liquid soon dried. The wounded flesh was a greenish color with flashes of gold—it was a strange color. Steam began to rise from it. It may have been an illusion, but Jūkichi thought he smelled a rotting odor.

Jūkichi returned the animal to the water, in the same position it had been originally, with the head toward the shore and the tail toward the sea.

The *naméso* allowed Jūkichi to do as he pleased.

Jūkichi climbed back into his boat. He took out his pipe. He took two or three puffs and drank some lukewarm water. His body was covered with salt. There was no fresh water to rinse it off. He lay down in the bottom of the boat. He was exhausted from the exertion. For a short while, he slept.

When he awoke, the *naméso* hadn't moved.

It will probably die, he thought.

It's a naméso, *so why should I care if it dies*, he thought.

The current was changing. Though he was not unconcerned about the *naméso*, he pushed his boat off the shore with his pole. He'd be in big trouble if he missed the current. He had to catch one current after another to get back, like jumping from one stepping stone to the next.

When he'd reached open water, he looked back at the *naméso*.

The beach was white and the water at the shore was a golden tint. The *naméso* looked like a large piece of driftwood that had washed ashore.

The next day Jūkichi left the harbor while it was still dark.

He wanted to get to Iwanejima. He headed straight there, without stopping anywhere else.

He thought that the *naméso* was probably dead. He hoped he wouldn't find its corpse. If it was going to die, he hoped it would go out into the open sea to do so. And if that was the case, there was no reason to go all the way to Iwanejima.

But he had to know what happened.

He reached the island at daybreak. He headed straight toward the beach. As he approached, he noticed that there was no sign of the *naméso*. The beach was a stretch of pure white.

Sculling up to near the shore, Jūkichi stopped his boat.

He was relieved. He felt it would have been terrible to discover the corpse. He decided it must have gone out to sea and died there. Or maybe it recovered and swam away.

He decided to forget about the whole thing.

He questioned why, in spite of being a fisherman, he had nursed the naméso. He felt a kind of regret for his actions. But at the same time, he also missed the creature. Even if it had recovered, they would never meet again. They were separated by the unbridgeable barrier dividing those who live on land and those who live in water. Yet in spite of that divide, he felt something.

He waited an hour for the current.

Rising to pull up the anchor, Jūkichi gasped.

Out of nowhere, the *naméso* had appeared. Its black body was swimming up alongside the boat.

Jūkichi was dumbstruck. Frozen, he just sat there staring for some time.

The *naméso* had remembered him—that's what he thought. There was no other explanation. *Naméso* are wary sea beasts. They would never approach a boat under normal circumstances; that would mean their death. Such a stunt could only mean that this *naméso* remembered him.

A chill ran down his spine.

Finally Jūkichi moved. He kneeled against the gunwale.

"You...you...waited for me?"

He reached out and touched it.

The *naméso* began to swim slowly. It swam around the boat and back to the original spot. It lifted its head from the water and called out. It screeched *Ki-ki, ki-ki,* like a mouse.

"Wait, wait," Jūkichi said excitedly. With his net, he scooped up some horse mackerel he had for bait. He held it out for the *naméso*. The *naméso* took it nimbly. Jūkichi was completely engrossed. He gave all twenty-four horse mackerel to the *naméso*.

The *naméso* retreated. It swam around the boat again, then headed slowly out for deep water. Its black form disappeared in the sea.

Jūkichi stood up and watched it go. He continued to look after it for some time after its departure.

When he sat down again, he sighed heavily. His fingertips were trembling with emotion. It was clear that the *naméso* had been waiting for Jūkichi. The *naméso* hadn't been panting when he found it yesterday because of the pain of the wound. It had been exhausted from becoming entangled in the net. It hadn't called out asking Jūkichi to treat its wound. It had been pleading, "Don't kill me…Let me live."

Overnight, the *naméso* had regained its strength. It could have just disappeared. But the *naméso* had waited.

Or perhaps Jūkichi just happened to arrive at the moment when the *naméso* was about to swim off.

Jūkichi took out his saké flask. His legs were shaking. The center brace across the boat's hull was said to be the dwelling place of the boat's spirit. He poured some saké for the boat's spirit. He did this every morning before he went out to sea.

Jūkichi observed the rite, but he had never believed in the existence of gods or Buddhas.

Maybe they do exist, he thought for the first time.

He raised his head. The *naméso*'s eyes looked like the eyes of someone, he thought. He didn't know whose. He wasn't able to reach back that far to the indistinct memory in his distant past.

That day he returned to the harbor after noon.

"Why are you back so early?" Ishi asked suspiciously.

"No reason."

"No?" asked Ishi perfunctorily.

From way back, Jūkichi would at times appear to be in a kind of daze. Sometimes he even seemed to be suffering from a high fever. That's how he looked now.

He was an unremarkable man. He'd never gotten into a fight or argument. He'd always been firmly under Ishi's control. Up to now, she'd always managed to make him do as she pleased. She'd do so until he died.

It had never occurred to Ishi that Jūkichi might have special feelings about anything.

Jūkichi left the harbor again the next day before dawn.

As he rode the current, Jūkichi's deeply wrinkled face glowed. His few white hairs blowing in the predawn sea wind seemed rejuvenated.

A new, green sprout was emerging from the weary, brown clump of his withered heart. Jūkichi could smell its fragrance.

There was no possibility that the *naméso* would be there to greet him again. The *naméso* had already sufficiently expressed its gratitude for Jūkichi's benevolence and had swum away. It was now plunging forward to join its fellow creatures far out to sea.

That was to be expected, and that was what Jūkichi wanted to happen.

"I hope I never set eyes on that *naméso* again," pledged Jūkichi silently. The *naméso* was the fisherman's loathsome enemy, now and forever. True as that might be, Jūkichi couldn't agree. Jūkichi had seen something resembling human emotion in the hated *naméso*. An animal that could communicate emotionally with a human being could not be an enemy. Hating the *naméso* would be the same as hating people. Killing a *naméso* would be the same as killing a person.

That's how Jūkichi felt.

The light of the just-risen sun struck the beach of Iwanejima. The water at the shore line was a jade color. The sunlight reflected off the white sand and was shimmering in what seemed to be a band of very faint rising mist.

Jūkichi sat down on the beach. He looked out to sea. In the distance, he could see the island on which he lived. It was a small island resembling a seated camel. The two ends of the island were deeply indented. It looked like something had taken a bite out of them. The local weather and winds, especially in summer, had eroded the land. People said the island had been eaten by summer insects.

The island looked like it was floating, unanchored, on the sea.
There was no *naméso*.

It was as he'd expected. The *naméso* had gone off in pursuit of its own kind. Jūkichi felt nothing in particular. He had treated the *naméso* the day before yesterday. The *naméso* had come to greet him yesterday. There was a connection between the day before yesterday and yesterday. The *naméso* had merely come to this uninhabited island to heal. Jūkichi had just happened to encounter it before it left on its journey.

And now the *naméso* had gone.

There was no connection between yesterday and today.

Jūkichi had come to the island knowing that full well. For two days he'd experienced a feeling of heightened emotion, as if a miracle or a dream were unfolding before his eyes. He felt something burning within him. That was enough, he thought.

Jūkichi knew he didn't have that much longer to live. Though only a few years remained to him, he'd treasure his memories of the *naméso* until his life came to its end.

He sat there idly turning these thoughts over in his mind.

Something was happening in the water. Lost in thought, Jūkichi hadn't noticed. When he finally did, he could clearly see that something peculiar was going on.

There were ripples in the water off the beach. There was no wind. There were no waves. The sea was as clear as a mirror. One area in the water, however was roiling. The ripples formed a line about fifty meters long. It was like a giant log had floated up from the ocean bottom. The black ripple was moving with great speed toward the beach.

Jūkichi rose to his feet. He had never seen anything like it.

With astonishing speed, the black ripple hit the beach.

Jūkichi retreated. He didn't know what it was, but it seemed ominous. There was something threatening about that black ripple moving at remarkable speed.

When he had rushed halfway up the beach, the ripple behind him broke, making a loud noise.

Jūkichi turned around to look.

He opened his eyes buried deep in his wrinkles.

A huge school of fish was flopping on the white sand beach. It was a school of several thousand horse mackerel. Twenty or thirty large kisslip squid were mixed in with them. The beach was alive with moving fish. The mackerel, regretting their rush up onto the beach, were flopping around, making a rippling sound as they danced wildly on the sand.

The squid also clearly regretted their situation. They kept changing their color, as if trying to fool themselves. Squid have the ability to match their color to their surroundings. But they couldn't match the pure white of the sand. In a panic, they were turning a purplish black, exerting their powers to the limit.

Jūkichi thought that the squid must have chased the school of horse mackerel. The mackerel, with no escape in sight, sought refuge on land in their extreme terror. This was the first time Jūkichi had observed this, but it was a well-known phenomena.

There was one thing he didn't understand, however. Why had the squid also leaped up onto the beach? He'd never heard of the pursuing fish following their prey onto land. No animal chased their pray so relentlessly that they lost their bearings to that extent.

Suddenly the sea surface parted.

It was the *naméso*. It lifted its body half out of the water and called, *Ki-ki, ki-ki!* shaking its head.

Jūkichi looked at the *naméso*, dumbfounded. It was singing a victory song. It dived down again, rose up through the surface, and called out.

The *naméso* sparkled in the morning sun. Its back was black and its belly white. It was a brilliant contrast. Most fish are of similar coloration. When viewed from above, the dark color blends in with the sea's depths, and when viewed from below, their pale underside matches the light at the water's surface.

Both pursuers and pursued shared this coloration. The biological name for it is counter shading.

The *naméso* was singing.

Having come to his senses again, Jūkichi rushed to his boat. He grabbed his net and began retrieving the kisslip squid. One of the boat's fish wells was soon filled with squid. He dumped the horse mackerel into another well.

He only netted up a few of the mackerel. He couldn't do anything about the rest. He filled his net and sculled out in the boat.

The *naméso* swam up to him. It stuck its head up at the side of the boat. Jūkichi fed it mackerel.

He placed the fish in the *naméso*'s mouth one at a time. As he did so, he wept. He was all choked up, overcome with sadness. As for why he felt this way, Jūkichi had no clear idea.

The *naméso* ate until it was full.

It swam under the boat, playing, then leaped out of the water. Looking at Jūkichi with its round eyes, it cried out. Its voice was high and clear.

Jūkichi sat on the gunwale, watching it. His body felt as heavy as someone with a serious illness.

The *naméso* gradually swam off, calling as it did so.

Jūkichi remained motionless, looking in the direction the *naméso* went, long after it had disappeared.

Fear pressed in on Jūkichi's heart.

The kisslip squid had leaped up onto the beach because they were being pursued by the *naméso*. The kisslip squid had been chasing the horse mackerel, and the *naméso* the squid.

Jūkichi knew that it had been a coincidence. He was fully aware that the *naméso* hadn't chased the fish up onto the beach to thank him.

But Jūkichi attributed a disturbingly profound significance to this coincidence. He felt the need to recast this coincidence into an inevitability.

The *naméso* had lost its sense of where to go.

That's what frightened Jūkichi. Jūkichi couldn't understand why it didn't try to rejoin the others of its kind. Its injury had healed, and now the time had come for it to swim off to the open sea. It had been many years since *naméso* had disappeared from the polluted waters of these parts. This *naméso* was one of a herd that had, for some reason, been swimming through the Inland Sea on their way to somewhere else. While chasing fish, it'd gotten caught in a net. The other *naméso* didn't think they could save it, so they left without it and went on their way.

Maybe this was still a baby *naméso*. Maybe it didn't have the ability to follow its herd and rejoin with them.

If that was so, Jūkichi had done something very serious. By treating the *naméso*, he had interacted with it. The result was that the *naméso* had lost its fear of human beings. Jūkichi knew exactly what would happen to a *naméso* that had lost its fear of humans, of fishermen.

He could see the *naméso* swimming up to another boat, mistaking it for his. Or coming up to another fisherman, thinking that people were playmates.

He could see the bloody pulp to which the *naméso* would be reduced. He could see it dead, a gaff through its head, before it even had a chance to doubt that the other human was its friend.

Jūkichi looked out to sea with a gloomy expression. He didn't know what to do.

He hoped that the *naméso* would swim off today. He hoped so fervently. Until it did, he would make his way to Iwanejima every day, filled with foreboding. The day would come when the *naméso*'s trust of humans would be destroyed. Even if that didn't happen, winter would be here soon. In winter, the waves were high even in the Inland Sea. There would be many days when Jūkichi wouldn't be able to go out fishing.

Would the *naméso* continue to wait around for him even then, he wondered.

Jūkichi's heart was heavy, as if he'd swallowed a stone.

He looked up.

Something made its way dimly through his thoughts.

"Tōru," he whispered.

The other day, it had struck Jūkichi that the round eyes of the *naméso* reminded him of someone. He didn't know who. Now he remembered. They were Tōru's eyes.

Tōru was Jūkichi's only son. He had been drafted the year before the war ended. He never came back. No image of him remained in Jūkichi's mind. But the sight of his round eyes as a boy sometimes came back to Jūkichi.

The *naméso*'s eyes resembled Tōru's.

Behold the dawn on the eastern sea
When the morning sun shines from on high
It clearly reveals the truth of heaven and earth.

Jūkichi sang in his gravelly voice. It was the only song he ever sang. When Tōru went off to war, the villagers saw him off to the ferry. The village headman gave a speech, and after Tōru made a few remarks in reply, the head of the village military committee, a former naval sergeant major, sang the song in a ringing voice.

Since then, Jūkichi sometimes sang the song when he was out at sea, tears falling from his eyes.

By now he had forgotten the lyrics.

"*Naméso*," said Jūkichi after he'd finished singing. "Have you brought Tōru's spirit to me from the southern seas? Are you Tōru reborn?"

"Tōru—"

Jūkichi looked at the sea, his eyes dry.

Jūkichi didn't sell the kisslip squid.

They were the highest quality squid. He would have made more than one hundred thousand yen if he'd sold them. But it would also have meant exposing his secret. It was rare to catch kisslip squid. He knew that people would have been suspicious.

He kept going to Iwanejima every day. He spent his days as if in the grip of a fever. It didn't bother him that Ishi was growing more and more irritated with each passing day.

The *naméso* came to see Jūkichi every day. Sometimes Jūkichi had to wait several hours before it arrived.

Jūkichi fed it kisslip squid. The *naméso* called out happily. Jūkichi petted its head. He put his hand into its mouth, with its tiny, neatly arranged teeth. The *naméso* didn't bite.

Jūkichi realized that the old story that a human child's foot had been found in a *naméso*'s stomach was a lie.

The deeper their relationship grew, the heavier Jūkichi's heart became. The *naméso* showed no signs of leaving Iwanejima. *What was it thinking*, Jūkichi wondered. *Why didn't it leave Iwanejima? Why didn't it try to rejoin the other* naméso*?*

Jūkichi was afraid that eventually the *naméso* would come looking for him and follow him back to the harbor.

Maybe it was still young and unable to find the others. Or perhaps the pollution of the Inland Sea had done something to interfere with its natural homing instinct.

Jūkichi watched the water, the color of which looked increasingly more melancholy.

The loon had watched Jūkichi struggle with the Spanish mackerel. Its shiny red eyes seemed somehow scornful.

It stayed by the side of the boat. Continuing his struggle with the Spanish mackerel long after he was tired of it, Jūkichi also watched the loon. There was just the one bird. No others. He thought it was the same loon that had been there when Jūkichi discovered the wounded, exhausted *naméso*.

It was a ravenous loon, and curious too. Discovering the wounded *naméso*, it had looked at it quizzically.

Perhaps this loon had also lost its flock. Maybe like the *naméso*, it had forgotten how to get home, and was there floating on the sea all alone. And like the *naméso*, it always appeared from out of nowhere and then hung around Jūkichi's boat.

Finally the Spanish mackerel began to tire.

Jūkichi was weary too. As he pulled the fish in, he looked at the current. It was changing. He had fought with the mackerel too long. If he kept it up, he wouldn't make it to Iwanejima. And if he sculled to Iwanejima without the current, he wouldn't get back to harbor until the middle of the night.

The *naméso* waiting for him was in the back of his mind.

He was pulling in the Spanish mackerel. It was close enough that he could see its dark form vaguely in the cloudy sea. Jūkichi rushed. He drew the line in by force. Jūkichi had never fished this way before. He brought his fish up gradually, accustoming them to the change in water pressure, so that their swim bladders didn't rupture. If the swim bladder ruptured, you had to make a hole in it with a needle. He didn't force the fish up, which is why his catch was always perfect, every scale intact.

But in his rush, he broke his own rules.

The form of the fish passed under his boat. Jūkichi grabbed his big scoop net. He pulled in the fish, swimming speedily at an angle, applying his full strength. The mackerel must have been five feet long. He caught the mackerel in the scoop net. Jūkichi put his back into it. It was a familiar stance for him. With the line tight in his left hand, he pulled up the scoop net with his right.

The fish leaped into the air. The sun glistened on its teeth. It was a huge fish with a face like a demon. Its weight brought Jūkichi down.

He let out a cry. The fish, sparkling in the sun, fell on top of Jūkichi. It slipped out of the scoop net.

Jūkichi fell. The mackerel landed on his left leg. He felt a sharp pain. Jūkichi crawled away. His foot was bloody. The mackerel's teeth, sharper than razors, had ripped a wound in his calf about four inches long. He didn't know how deep it was. Blood was pouring out of it.

3

Jūkichi must have gone senile and lost his mind, thought Ishi.

This was his fourth day in bed. He had come home wounded. He said that he'd tripped and cut himself with his axe, but the nurse who treated him at the clinic said that it looked like he'd been bitten by a mackerel. He'd been fishing for mackerel, so that made sense.

When a fisherman is bitten by a fish, it's all over for him.

On top of that, Jūkichi had a fever. He talked to himself while he was sleeping. He didn't eat. Ishi listened to try to discover what he was saying in his sleep. There must be some reason that Jūkichi was no longer catching any fish.

Jūkichi murmured, "It's the *naméso*" and "It's Tōru." Ishi was disgusted. Jūkichi still couldn't accept his son's death. It gave her the creeps to think of him going out to sea, just sitting there all day without fishing, thinking of their son who'd died thirty years ago.

Jūkichi, she concluded, wasn't long for this world.

When she thought of how hard it would be for her after he died, she hated him for his weakness and senility.

On the fourth day, Ishi had had enough.

"Pull yourself together, old man. It's shameful for you to sit around thinking of your dead child."

"I'm sorry, Ishi."

"Sorry isn't enough." Once she got angry, Ishi wasn't easily mollified.

Jūkichi was silent.

Ishi was wearing a loose shift, revealing her drooping, shriveled, yellow breasts.

"This has gone far enough!" she said, leaving the house.

Jūkichi looked up at the rafters. Spider webs hung from the sooty ceiling. He was anxious. This was the fourth day. And he hadn't been to the island the day he was injured, so it was the fifth day.

"What's the *naméso* doing?"

He felt a prickling apprehension.

The *naméso* must be waiting for him. Day after day it must have waited for the shadow of his boat.

But Jūkichi never arrived.

What must the *naméso* have thought? Did it miss him? Or was that something only humans felt?

Jūkichi closed his eyes.

The next day, he went out to sea.

His wound was starting to heal. He'd been told he shouldn't move for another two or three days. But he couldn't stay still. If it had just been the wound, he'd have gone out on his boat the day before, but his fever had prevented that. This morning, his fever was gone.

He headed toward Iwanejima.

There was no sign of anything on the sandy beach of Iwanejima. Jūkichi stopped his boat. He was nearly overwhelmed by a feeling of desolation. The sea looked somehow different.

The first signs of autumn were making themselves known on the late summer sea. The change of seasons was visible in the color of the waves. Just slightly, the sea was blackening. The wind blew ripples that had a cold look. Just five days earlier, the ripples had felt lax and lazy.

The sunshine striking the white sand seemed weaker. A piece of driftwood with thin branches lay on the beach. The tips of the branches were quivering in an almost undetectable breeze. This was a harbinger of autumn.

Jūkichi had made the mugwort pulp just two weeks ago. In that two weeks, summer had lost its intensity.

Jūkichi looked out to sea. He looked at the beach.

It was a dead scene. Maybe ruined was a better description. It seemed drained of all life. It had a coldness that suggested it would never be resurrected.

He waited, though he had no idea for what. What could he be waiting for from this dead sea before his eyes?

Jūkichi stayed there in his boat until the sun had set.

When it was dark, he stood up.

He didn't know what had happened to the *naméso*. Perhaps it had given up on Jūkichi after he'd failed to appear, and it had gone off to join its kind. Or perhaps it had approached some other fishing boat and fallen victim to a gaff. Or maybe it had gotten caught in a net, been butchered at a fish market, and was now an ingredient in *kamaboko*. Jūkichi's legs were exhausted. He returned home late that night.

"Did you catch anything?" asked Ishi with concern.

"I can't."

"What do you mean, you can't?"

"Ishi," said Jūkichi, looking directly at her, as he rarely did. "Why don't you go fishing tomorrow?"

"'*You* go fishing?' You mean, *me*?"

"Yes."

"I can't believe what I'm hearing!" She was dumbfounded.

There was something unyielding in Jūkichi's face. She'd never seen this before. His chin was firm. His eyes beneath his long, white eyebrows were cold and determined. Ishi shivered.

"I can't believe what I'm hearing!" she gulped, repeating herself. "If you can't fish, what good are you? How can you even say that?" she gasped. "You haven't heard the end of this."

"Do as you like," said Jūkichi coldly.

It was cloudy the next morning.

Jūkichi knew that when the tide returned in the afternoon it would rain.

Jūkichi approached Iwanejima, and from there caught one current after another. Nearby was the island with the best fishing in the area. It was busy throughout the year, with sea bream and

Spanish mackerel netting in the spring, then sand eel, butterfish, squid, and cutlass fish later in the year.

Jūkichi visited the fishing cooperative there. He asked if anyone had caught a *naméso* in the last few days, or reported seeing one.

They were puzzled by his question.

Jūkichi got back in his boat and began sculling.

It started raining before he'd reached Iwanejima. It was a hard rain that quickly obscured his field of vision. The sea was covered with white breakers. Jūkichi was soaked as he worked the scull.

Suddenly he noticed something swimming in the breakers. It was next to the boat. Jūkichi's pulse quickened. It must be the *naméso*, he thought. It had appeared alongside the boat and was now swimming next to him.

Jūkichi let go of the scull and leaned over the side of the boat.

It was a large loggerhead turtle. The turtle was swimming desperately through the high waves, trying to get somewhere.

He arrived at Iwanejima at evening. The island was rained in. Jūkichi took the horse mackerel he'd bought in case he found the *naméso* and scooped them up with his net. He waited for them to die, and then threw them into the sea.

He directed his boat toward home.

The next two days he went to Iwanejima. The white bodies of the dead horse mackerel were floating uselessly off the beach.

On the fourth day, Jūkichi began fishing.

He'd decided not to worry about the *naméso*. It must have swum out to the open sea, he concluded. If it had headed east, it might have passed from the Tomogashima Strait through the Kii Strait. If it had gone west, it may have passed through the Bungo Strait. It had waited several days for Jūkichi, and then given up. He was relieved. If the *naméso* had regained its natural instincts, it would be safe. Its only natural enemy might be orca. *Naméso* were rarely caught by people. It would join its herd and live out its natural life in peace.

Its interaction with Jūkichi was, in the end, a relationship between a human being and an animal. It couldn't last.

It was good that he'd been injured by the Spanish mackerel. If he hadn't been hurt, he and the *naméso* would still have been wasting each other's time. Jūkichi had been drawn to Iwanejima as if bewitched. It was only natural Ishi should be angry. A fisherman who couldn't fish was, as she said, worthless.

Things had worked out for the best for both of them, he thought.

When he started fishing again, Ishi's attitude changed.

She had always treated him like dirt. She cursed and belittled him on a daily basis. Jūkichi never stood up to her. He couldn't have beat her in an argument if he had tried.

But now Ishi addressed him in ingratiating tones. She decided that charm was more effective than cursing. She'd received quite a scare, it seemed. It was a tremendous change. Jūkichi smiled to himself coldly.

The change in Ishi was the one gift the *naméso* had left for him. A sadness raced through his heart.

What was that *naméso*? People said they were finless porpoises or dolphins, but Jūkichi didn't think they were either.

He was no longer even certain the encounter had really happened. It was such an exceptional event that now, those extraordinary days past, his memories were starting to grow fuzzy and dim.

Jūkichi began to offer a little more saké than usual to the spirit of his boat.

The sea had grown darker by mid-September.

The languor of summer was gone. The shadows cast by the clouds were deepening.

Nearly a month had passed since Jūkichi had encountered the *naméso*. It was more than a half-month since he had last seen it.

Jūkichi was concentrating on his fishing. He was after butterfish. His results were good. He hadn't forgotten the *naméso*, but he didn't go out of his way to recall it, either. He didn't have to; it was always there, at the back of his mind. But he no longer had any strong feelings about what had happened.

He saw the loon from time to time. The loon was always cruising around on its own. It occasionally came up to his boat. The pupils of its glossy red eyes were never visible, and it always seemed a bad omen to Jūkichi.

One day it seemed to be looking at Jūkichi. He had caught a lot of fish that day. He had just pulled up his sixth butterfish since the morning. He had no desire to catch a seventh. He might have been able to, but the change of the current was pressing in on him. He was at an age when he shouldn't be greedy.

He stood up, planning to wind up his fishing line.

He fell back. He grabbed the oar to steady himself.

Ki-ki! Ki-ki! Ki-ki!

A high voice rose from behind him. Jūkichi's heart seemed to stop. He couldn't breathe. The blood drained from his face and he looked out to sea.

The *naméso* was off in the distance, standing up in the water. Undulating its body to remain half out of water, it was calling him. Rather than calling, it seemed to be shouting at him. The sharp voice echoed over the water.

The *naméso*'s body fell back into the sea. A white splash rose from the blue water. The *naméso* was swimming. It had a unique manner of swimming. It dived and then occasionally sent its body out of the water. Its body was smooth and glistening. That's how it got its name.

It swam directly toward Jūkichi.

Jūkichi's legs were shaking so violently that he couldn't stand. He crouched on the edge of the boat. The *naméso* rose suddenly from the depths to the edge. Water splashed into the boat.

"It's you, it's you!" Jūkichi stroked the *naméso*'s head. His voice was shaking. His hand stroking the animal was shaking. The *naméso* looked at Jūkichi with its little round eyes. They seemed happy to Jūkichi.

"I can't believe it, I can't believe it's you!"

Jūkichi had no idea what he was saying. With his shaking hand he cut up the butterfish he'd just caught. He fed it to the *naméso*.

The *naméso* consumed it greedily. It shook its head happily as it ate.

After eating two butterfish, the *naméso* dived beneath the boat. It appeared on the other side, dancing on the water's surface. Jūkichi was doused with spray. He didn't even wipe away the water that splashed his face, but just sat there grasping the edge of the boat, watching the *naméso*. Like a child playing hide and seek, the *naméso* disappeared.

After a short time, the *naméso* surfaced far off in the distance, projecting its body above the water. It called, made a splash, and disappeared beneath the waters.

Jūkichi stared. The *naméso* swam to the right and then to the left. It stopped, raised its body out of the water, and called. It seemed to be trying very hard to communicate. It seemed to Jūkichi like an expression of uncontrollable joy.

It was a very energetic performance, and watching it Jūkichi realized that the *naméso* had grown stronger. As it broke through the water and danced above the waves, it seemed like a powerful warrior.

The *naméso* kept swimming. Tracing a large circle around the boat, it went round and round. From time to time it raised itself out of the water and looked at Jūkichi.

Jūkichi could hardly see.

His heart was filled with emotion and anxiety. The emotion was from the realization that the *naméso* had been looking for him. They were quite a ways from Iwanejima. The *naméso* had been searching intensively for Jūkichi. It's no easy thing to find a single small boat in the vast expanse of the sea.

A half-month had passed since his parting with the *naméso*. The *naméso* may have been looking for Jūkichi for much of the time in those weeks after Jūkichi had given up his search for it.

This exuberant dance was proof of that.

Though initially overjoyed at this unexpected encounter, Jūkichi was soon overcome with fear.

The *naméso* had been away from Iwanejima for almost ten days. That was certain. Where had it gone? From its speed, it could have traveled a considerable distance in ten days. The *naméso* had been looking for its kind.

But they weren't to be found.

The *naméso* had to turn back.

This frenzied behavior was an expression of the *naméso*'s loneliness.

The loneliness that forced it to return to a human being—that's what the *naméso* was expressing with its entire body.

Why don't you go out to sea, asked Jūkichi silently. *There are no others of your kind here. What good can come from you returning to a fisherman? There's nothing for you here. You need to make your home in the sea. I can't live in the sea. Why? Why did you come back?*

Jūkichi was weeping.

In the distance, the *naméso* was calling.

Its voice pierced Jūkichi like a sharp needle.

In the distance, a ferryboat glided by like a white limestone castle.

4

The slack water between high and low tides is called *daré*.

Two boats were trolling the *daré* with a net. A purse seine. The net was attached to both boats, which gradually pulled it tight, just like you'd pull the mouth of a purse tight.

They were fishing for butterfish.

They hadn't caught anything that day. They'd put out their net several times, but had hardly caught a thing.

Usually there are more fish when the tide is strong. People rarely use nets in slack water. But these fishermen hadn't been catching anything that day, and they were impatient. So as evening was approaching, they cast their net into the slack water.

The dozen or so young fishermen in the two boats tightened the purse seine, calling out to each other to stay in rhythm.

The sun was setting in the sea between the mainland and Shikoku.

The colors of sunset tinted the boats and the bare-chested young men.

"Huh? What? What's that?!" one of the young fisherman called out when they had the net about eight-tenths closed. The two boats were aligned next to each other. The net was between them. If there had been a large catch in the net, the fish would start panicking as the net closed, forming schools rising up and down in the water.

But the net was quiet.

They thought they had caught nothing again. Not a single little fish was swimming in the net. It was just a bunch of jellyfish. And one large thing was floating in their midst. Something deep black. The fishermen started shouting. The sea was already dark. The water was even darker. They looked fearfully into the darkness below them.

Before the large thing revealed its identity, it silently dived.

The calls of the fishermen grew louder as they closed the net in one final pull.

"It's a *naméso*! The bastard!"

A single *naméso* was inside the tightly closed purse seine. It was the only thing in the net.

"It's this one's fault! That's why there are no fish in our net!"

"Kill it!" the fishermen all started shouting.

The aggravation of the fishermen, who had expected a catch of several dozen butterfish, was concentrated on the lone *naméso* inside their net, partly because they hadn't caught anything all day.

Several fishermen grabbed long-handled gaffs to kill the beast. The poles were six feet long and topped by a sharp, curving hook more than five inches long.

"Son of a bitch!"

One of them struck the *naméso* in the back.

The *naméso* cried out, screeching *Kii-kii*.

The net was completely closed and being pulled out of the water. Blood spurted from its back.

"This fucker!" With that cry, another hook fell on the *naméso*.

"What should we do, Captain?" asked one of the fishermen.

"Throw it in the fish well," said the captain angrily.

They could sell it at the fish market to be ground up for *kamaboko*. It would be childish to just kill it and leave it there.

The *naméso* was pulled into the live well with three long gaffs. Net-fishing boats have large live wells. When they catch fish, they put a top on the well and fill it with sea water. At other times, the live well is drained and has a top over it. If it was always filled with water, the boat would be heavier and harder to move.

The *naméso* was thrown into the live well without any water.

The fishermen folded up the nets as they headed back to the harbor.

When they arrived at the harbor, one of the fishermen looked into the live well with a battery-powered lamp.

The live well was a sea of blood. It was filled with blackish, sticky blood. The *naméso* was wriggling in the blood.

"You're a tough one. Still alive, huh?"

The fisherman was amazed at the beast's will to survive. Its back was sliced open by three strikes from gaff hooks. On top of that, it had remained in this live well for over an hour without any water. He thought it would be dead.

"It'll sell for more if it's still alive," said the captain. "Tie it up and throw it in the water."

One of the fisherman tied a rope around the *naméso*'s tail. Several of them worked together to drag it out of the live well and dump it in the sea.

"Go ahead, escape if you can. If you die, we'll cook and eat you. Take that."

The *naméso* sank to the bottom of the shallow water in the harbor and remained there, motionless.

Jūkichi arrived at the harbor.

It was dawn. There were many people there. It was almost time for the first ferry to depart for Takamatsu. The ferry pier was the only real gathering place on the island. People just came there and hung around, even if they weren't taking the ferry.

Jūkichi had no interest in people. With his bent back, he headed for the pier where his boat was tied up and got into it.

He poured an offering of saké for the spirit of the boat and untied the mooring rope. He pushed off with a pole, wet the scull mount, and began sculling out to sea.

Near the entry to the harbor a net-fishing boat with a purse-seine net was moored. A knot of people were gathered on the dock making a fuss over something.

Jūkichi sculled his boat close to the net-fishing boat.

The strange scene he saw made him weak in the knees. A rope ran down from the boat's stern. The rope was heading straight out to the entry to the harbor. At the end of the rope was a black beast. It was daybreak. You couldn't see clearly. But you could see it wasn't a fish. If it wasn't a fish—

At that instant, Jūkichi's blood went cold. His skin became like stone and lost all pliability. The blood drained from his extremities and his entire body was as cold as ice.

The *naméso*.

He felt dizzy. He found himself tipping over, and it seemed as if he might fall into the water. He let go of the scull and crawled to the prow. The boat floated lazily in the water.

"It's, it's y-y-y-y-you!" screamed Jūkichi. It was the *naméso*. The strips of flesh along the wounds opened like flower petals. The *naméso* was swimming with all its might. With its head directed toward the entry to the harbor, it was swimming, undulating its body. The rope cut into its tail. It kept rising to the surface and sinking down again.

The *naméso* saw Jūkichi. It looked at him sadly with its little round eyes.

"You!" Jūkichi screamed.

The *naméso* seemed to recognize Jūkichi. It stopped its desperate swimming and floated to the surface, as if exhausted. It came to the side of his boat.

Jūkichi stood up. He tore off his clothes. Wearing only his loincloth, he grabbed his hand axe.

The people watching the *naméso* on the pier gasped. They thought Jūkichi was going to kill the *naméso*. The *naméso* was a hated enemy of all fishermen, of the whole fishing village. But that still didn't mean you had to jump into the ocean and kill it.

They thought Jūkichi had lost his mind.

Jūkichi jumped into the water with a splash.

Jūkichi cut the rope with his axe. He embraced the *naméso*. With his boat's mooring line in his teeth, still embracing the *naméso*, he headed for the beach. The *naméso* let Jūkichi carry it along. It seemed to have expended all its body heat. It was cold, enveloped by a sticky membrane.

When debilitated, sea animals secrete a sticky membrane from their skin. It hangs from them like strings. Once that stage is reached, the end is near. The *naméso* seemed to have exuded all its bodily fluids.

Jūkichi's body was on fire. A wild and uncontrollable force was driving him.

The people watched, dumbfounded. Jūkichi didn't kill the *naméso*. He was swimming with it, his arms around it. And he was pulling his boat with the mooring rope in his teeth. They couldn't imagine what was going on.

Naméso were supposed to be fierce and dangerous. But Jūkichi, almost naked, had his arms around it.

When they realized Jūkichi was heading for the shore, they all dashed there in a mad rush.

Jūkichi rested the *naméso* on the beach.

Three deep wounds from the gaffing hooks cut into its back. They were vicious gashes, deep enough to stick a fist into.

"You…you…" Jūkichi dragged himself up on to the beach and stroked the *naméso*'s head. He didn't know what to say. Tears poured from his eyes. He'd just been reunited with the *naméso* the day before. The *naméso* had played with him for almost an hour.

They had parted late in the afternoon.

Had the *naméso* come after Jūkichi?

The people came running up. But they didn't approach Jūkichi. They formed a ring around him, some distance off.

The morning sun dyed the sea golden.

One man stepped out from the ring of onlookers.

"What are you doing, old man?"

It was the captain of the net-fishing boat. He addressed Jūkichi in a puzzled tone. "Where do you get off stealing my *naméso*?"

Jūkichi stood, holding the axe.

"'*My*' *naméso*?"

The captain took two or three steps back. Jūkichi was a strange sight. He was thin and small, and his testicles had fallen out of his loincloth. But frail as he was, his body steamed with rage.

"I'll kill you!" shouted Jūkichi, waving the axe. He ran up on the beach.

The people retreated.

The captain retreated, too. Looking behind him at Jūkichi, he ran away.

"Are you crazy, old man?" he shouted as he fled.

Jūkichi had never fought or argued in his life. He was one of those invisible men, one of those men who made no impression, good or bad.

Jūkichi stopped his pursuit. He returned to the *naméso*.

"What do you think you're doing!?" A piercing voice rang out from the crowd.

It was Ishi. She ran out.

"Get out of here, you shit-faced hag!" screamed Jūkichi.

"What are you doing with that *naméso*—are you crazy?"

Ishi blanched and stopped in her tracks.

Jūkichi didn't reply.

"Come on! Say something!"

Ishi felt as if she was losing her mind. Jūkichi had gone mad. She was terrified.

"You don't have anything to say? Hey! What? Speak up!"

She shouted wildly, baring her teeth.

Jūkichi didn't hear her screams.

"I'll…I'll take care of you again," he said to the *naméso*, weeping.

One of the fishermen approached.

"What's going on, Jūkichi?"

It was an elderly fisherman named Yoshizō. If Jūkichi had a friend, it would have been Yoshizō.

"Look what they did to…my *naméso*." Jūkichi was crying.

"Is that your *naméso*?"

Yoshizō was beginning to understand. He could do nothing but accept Jūkichi's explanation at face value. Seeing Jūkichi weeping like this, his faced distorted in grief, he knew Jūkichi had not gone mad.

Speechless, Yoshizō stood there.

Jūkichi began to push the *naméso* back into the water. He tied it with a rope. He tied the rope to the edge of the boat.

Jūkichi climbed into the boat and, still naked, began to push the boat off with the pole. The *naméso* floated alongside the boat, making no attempt to move.

Jūkichi was sculling out toward the entrance to the harbor.

The morning sun cast its tint on his frail body.

There was a small beach on the northern coast of the island.

Jūkichi sat in a daze in the shallows.

The *naméso* was next to him. The waves moved its body ever so slightly. The *naméso* didn't move at all. It was looking at something with its small round eyes. *What*, Jūkichi wondered, *did it see?*

Maybe the realm of death. The *naméso* was wrapped in the shadow of death. Its skin was lifeless. It had lost the characteristic glossiness of a *naméso*. Even though it was in the water, it seemed dried out. The wounds where Jūkichi had applied the paste of mugwort and iodine were bluish green. They looked like they had already started to decay.

Maybe it was seeing the wide open sea, where the others of its kind lived, Jūkichi thought.

Death must have been this *naméso*'s destiny all along. That had been determined from the time it was separated from the others in its herd. After it had healed, it had spent several days looking for them. But no matter how far it swam, it couldn't find them. *Naméso* no longer lived in the badly polluted Inland Sea, unless they accidentally strayed into it.

The *naméso* gave up its search and came back.

Jūkichi vividly remembered the *naméso* when they had met again yesterday. Its wild joy when it had found Jūkichi again was burned into his brain.

Jūkichi's shoulders sagged.

He detested himself. He was unable even to save a single *naméso*. If he had any gumption, he would have cared for the *naméso* right there in the harbor. He would have convinced the villagers, found a veterinarian to treat the animal, and cared for it properly. But Jūkichi didn't have the verbal skills to convince the villagers.

If he had money, he could have done something. But he didn't have any money.

What a wasted life he'd lived.

A fishing boat approached.

It was Yoshizō's boat. Out of respect, Yoshizō tied the boat some distance away and walked along the beach to Jūkichi.

He sat down silently next to him.

"Do you think it will survive?" he asked after a brief silence.

"I don't know," said Jūkichi, shaking his head. "It may be too late." His voice was low and hoarse.

"I see."

Yoshizō took out a cigarette. He remained silent until he'd finished smoking it.

"So, what are you going to do?"

"I…" Jūkichi started to speak, but then closed his mouth. He sat there, silent for a long time.

"I became friends with this *naméso*. I'm an idiot. I know that. But I can't help it."

Jūkichi raised his head. A single loon was nearby. It was looking at him with its glossy, blood-red eyes.

He wanted to explain. It might have been the circumstances in which he met the *naméso*, it might have been that he was drawn to the *naméso*'s loneliness. But Jūkichi didn't possess the words to explain it.

The loon took flight. It flew in a straight line to the west, leaving a white wake in the water.

"I…" continued Jūkichi. "I'm going to take this *naméso* to the southern seas."

When he saw the direction the loon had flown, Jūkichi suddenly decided to take the *naméso* to the southern seas. He'd go west through the sea off Bingo, past Aki, and come out by Iyo. That would lead to the Bungo Channel.

If he took the Bungo Channel south, he'd come to the Pacific Ocean off Tosa. Jūkichi had never gone beyond the sea off of Bingo. The distance to that point and through the Bungo Channel to the Pacific was unimaginably long.

"Where in the southern ocean?"

"Off Tosa."

Jūkichi seemed to be looking off into the distance.

"All by sculling?"

"That's right."

"That's…that's ridiculous."

Yoshizō was shocked. To Yoshizō it seemed that the *naméso* was dying. The tide was just beginning to rise. The critical moment would be when it started to ebb. The end of life, for all beings, usually came with the ebbing of the tide. Living things didn't die when the tide was full.

The *naméso* would be dead before Jūkichi has sculled a league. Even if it didn't die, it was impossible to reach Tosa with a scull. If he tried, Jūkichi would die.

"Maybe it's ridiculous, but I'm going."

Jūkichi didn't believe it was impossible. It might take several months. He'd have to catch the currents, so he'd have to follow a roundabout route. But he had the time. He had all the time in the world. He'd fish as he went. If he bought rice and miso at ports along the way, he'd get to the south alive. He could sell the fish he caught along the way to buy miso and rice. For water, he could collect the rain.

If he stayed here, the *naméso* would die.

It might well die along the way. That would be fine. As long as it was still alive, the *naméso* was depending on him. It might even understand that he was taking it to the southern seas. Even if it died, it would probably be at least a little comforted that it was not alone.

And if, by some chance, it survived, that was all the more reason it couldn't remain in these waters. The *naméso* had to go out into the open sea. It had to go where there were others of its own kind.

I'm going, Jūkichi said to himself.

It was the only thing he could do.

It was the only way he could repay the *naméso*'s friendship.

If it died along the way, he'd take its corpse to the southern seas and lay it to rest in the pure, clean Japan Current.

"So. I'm going now."

Jūkichi stood up.

"Jūkichi, don't. You'll die."

He couldn't allow him to go. Yoshizō panicked.

"I don't expect to come back." Jūkichi smiled.

Seeing Jūkichi's smile, Yoshizo was speechless. It was a mysteriously serene smile.

Jūkichi stepped into the water up to his hips and placed the *naméso* inside the circle he'd made from the rope. The *naméso* allowed Jūkichi to do as he pleased with its body.

"Yoshizō…"

Jūkichi started to say something, then stopped.

He climbed up into the boat and dexterously used the pole to push off into the water.

Yoshizō crouched on the beach without moving, illuminated in the rays of the sun.

Jūkichi's boat moved off into the distance. Jūkichi worked the scull at an easy pace. The *naméso*'s large form was right next to the left side of the boat. In the light of the autumn sun, gradually the boat and Jūkichi grew smaller and smaller.

"Jūkichi," murmured Yoshizō, "Where do you think you're going?"

The Brave Crab

1

There was little night traffic on National Highway 128.

Trucker Masagoro Kaida was enjoying the extremely smooth driving. He'd left Tateyama in the evening. He was scheduled to make his delivery at Katsuura and return to Tateyama by morning.

September had just begun. The night air on the Boso Peninsula was still humid and warm. Kaida was wearing nothing but his boxers. The radio was on. He liked listening to the late-night broadcasts. The truck's headlights sliced through the darkness.

The shafts of light picked up a human form, what appeared to be a child. A boy was squatting in the middle of the highway. A dog sat next to him.

What could he be doing?

It was a little before 10:00 p.m. The surrounding area was wooded. There were no houses around. It was very odd for a boy and a dog to be crouched in the middle of the road. The boy was looking at the surface of the road with a flashlight. He was wearing a backpack.

Maybe he's a ghost, thought Kaida as he braked. They said that ghosts were often seen alongside the roads in Chiba on summer nights. People would see shifting white specters, or they would pick up a woman to give her a ride and then she'd suddenly disappear from the car.

Kaida was on guard, just in case this was some kind of poltergeist or vagrant spirit trying to play a trick on him.

He stopped the truck and yelled, "Hey!"

The boy and the dog completely ignored the roaring truck approaching them. They showed no reaction when he hit the horn. They just stayed where they were, squatting.

"Hey kid! What are you doing out here in the middle of the night?!" Kaida stepped out onto the highway. There was something strange about the boy and the dog. If they were ghosts, he'd send them back where they came from.

"I'm talking to you, kid!" said Kaida, grabbing the boy by the collar. He seemed to be about ten years old.

"Stop! Stop! My crab! My crab!" The boy pushed Kaida away. When Kaida released him, the boy immediately directed the flashlight beam back at the highway surface. Kaida's eyes followed it. A crab was crawling slowly sidewise. It brandished its bright red claws, extending both eyes on their stalks. It was in defense mode.

The dog sat and, tilting its head, watched the crab.

Kaida was stunned. At the same time, he was pissed off. A crab was crossing the highway. The boy and his dog saw it, were curious about it, and were watching it, oblivious to the fact that a truck was driving straight at them.

Where on earth had the boy come from, he wondered.

It was a red-clawed crab. They lived by the seashore. They made their homes in stone walls and piles of rubble. Some lived along rivers and streams. It wasn't a rare crab. Kaida was born and raised on the Boso Peninsula; he was quite familiar with them. The right and left claws were different in size. Usually the left claw was twice the size of the right. They caught their prey with the left, and then ripped off small pieces of flesh and placed them in their mouth with the smaller right claw.

The claws were bright red. Its body was also quite red. Their color made the crabs popular with kids.

That was all well and good, but a boy wearing a backpack and a dog crouched on the highway watching a crab crossing the road in the middle of the night was simply absurd.

The crab, its defenses still up, continued to crawl slowly across the road.

Several cars were approaching from the opposite direction—two passenger cars and two small trucks. Though 128 was designated a national highway, it was really nothing more than a narrow country road. The boy and the dog were in the middle of it. Kaida's large truck was, unavoidably, stopped in the middle of the road. There wasn't room to pass on either side. The vehicles had to stop. The drivers got out and approached.

"What happened?" asked the young man who had been driving the first passenger car.

"It's a crab. As you can see."

"What about the crab?" asked another, middle-aged man.

"How should I know?" replied Kaida curtly. "The crab was crossing the road. I suppose the boy and the dog found it. And now we're all stuck here. This kid paid no attention to my truck coming at him."

Both the boy and the dog ignored the adults. They moved slowly, along with the crab. The crab seemed to be tired.

"Hey, boy!" said the younger driver in a sharp voice. "Get that thing out of the way."

"No! The crab has to walk to the sea on his own," shouted the boy without looking up.

"The sea?!" The young man was angry. "The sea is kilometers away from here. Did you know that?"

"Of course I know that."

"You little brat! You want me to stomp on your crab?"

The man pushed the boy away. He made as if he was going to step on the crab.

When the dog saw this, it bared its fangs, growling.

The crab stopped crawling.

The boy hung onto the young man.

"Don't kill her! Don't kill her!"

"Let go of me!" He was really angry now. He grabbed the boy by the shirt and was about to hit him.

"Hey, stop that," said Kaida, peeling the young man off the boy. "You don't have to hit him. He's just a kid."

Kaida sensed something strange in the boy's outcry. He saw the boy's face in the headlights. It was covered with thick perspiration. Kaida had no idea what was going on, but it seemed clear that it was not just a case of a boy and a dog watching a crab they happened to discover crossing the highway.

"Then move the crab. I'm in a hurry."

"Why should I move it? It's not my crab."

"That's why *I* was trying to move it."

"You were trying to stomp on it."

"It's not your crab, so why should you care?" The young driver's voice was shaking.

"Anyway, there's no need to kill it."

"Then move it!"

"Why don't you try?" Kaida stepped between the crab and the young man. He didn't like this guy. He was in his mid-twenties. Just a glimpse at his hair and his clothes and you knew all you needed to know about him.

"Let's just all calm down," said the middle-aged driver, intervening. "There's no reason to let a little crab get us all into a fight, is there? When the crab moves, it'll all be over." His name was Ōno. He operated an inn in Shirahamamachi. He thought of himself as a reasonable man.

By that time, about ten cars were stopped behind Kaida's truck. Maybe twenty people were crowded around the boy, the dog, and the crab.

"Son," said Ōno, crouching down beside the boy. "Is that crab yours?"

"It belongs to me and Kuro," said the boy, still looking at the crab.

The crab stopped moving and began to foam at the mouth.

"What's your name?"

"Shin'ichi Todai. My dog is Kuro. The crab is Aka." The boy spoke very distinctly.

"How old are you?"

"Nine."

"Hurry it up! What are you screwing around for?" shouted the young driver.

"Why don't you just keep your mouth shut?" said Kaida, giving the guy a look.

"I'm in a hurry."

"So am I."

"This is a Uniform Traffic Ordinance violation, you know."

"Oh, so that's how it is. A college boy," snapped Kaida derisively, looking back at the boy, the dog, and the crab.

"Where's the crab going?" asked Ōno.

"To the sea, to lay its eggs."

"Oh, I see. It really does have a lot of eggs, doesn't it?" When he looked closely, he noticed that the crab had a large mass of pale lavender eggs adhering to its abdomen. It looked like it was resting because the eggs were so heavy. Maybe the foam was a sign of exertion.

"So, can you tell me one thing? Why don't you just take it to the sea?"

Everyone in the circle around the boy was watching. The crab rested, still, in the beam of Shin'ichi Todai's flashlight. Its eight legs were anchored on the asphalt. With its claws held up, it seemed very determined.

"Crabs have to make it to the sea on their own. People mustn't just take them there."

"Why?"

"Because, like Grandpa said, 'They'll lose their self-reliance.' He said it's the same with crabs and people. Red-clawed crabs lay their eggs in the sea on the nights of the full moon and the new moon in September and October. The first full moon is September 6. Aka knows that. That's why she's been walking, all on her own, for several days now, to get to the sea in time."

"You say she's been walking, all on her own, for several days now, to get to the sea in time. That means you—"

"Me and Kuro have come along with Aka since she first started. She's going straight to the sea. She just crosses any road in the way."

Ōno was silent.

"Kid," asked Kaida, "Where did you come from?"

"Way over there," replied Shin'ichi Todai, pointing inland. "At the foot of Mount Kompira. My grandpa said it was called Aono."

"The foot of Mount Kompira…Your crab walked here from there?" interjected Ōno.

Mount Kompira was in Awa County. From the foot of the mountain to here was six kilometers.

"Yeah. Over the mountains and through the woods."

"And you and the dog with her…"

"Yeah."

"But…" Ōno fell silent again. There were no roads in that area. That meant the boy, the dog, and the crab had walked through fields and over mountains for six kilometers.

"Kid, what's in your backpack?" asked Kaida.

"Food for me and Kuro. And a blanket and some other things."

"How long did it take you to get this far?"

"This is the fourth day since we left home."

"The fourth day—" Kaida looked at Ōno, who was busily searching his pockets for a cigarette. He finally managed to find one and placed it between his lips.

"That means," said Ōno, picking up the conversation, "that your grandpa told you and Kuro to go along with your crab…"

"Grandpa died."

"When?"

"Two nights before my crab left home."

"So someone else instead of your grandpa told you to go?"

"No," said Shin'ichi Todai, shaking his head. "Me and Kuro buried Grandpa, and then we just went with Aka. That's what my grandpa told me to do."

"Hey, wait a minute," chimed in Kaida. "Did you really bury your grandpa? You dug a hole?"

"You can't bury someone unless you dig a hole, pal," said Ōno, holding out the pack of cigarettes with some matches to Kaida. "Have a smoke. We've got a real mess on our hands here."

"What should we do?" asked Kaida, taking out a cigarette and putting it in his mouth.

Ōno looked around.

By this time about fifty cars were stopped on the road.

Ōno looked back at Kaida. "How are you at public speaking?"

"Public speaking?"

"Can you explain the situation to everyone in a loud voice? We'll just have to ask them to wait until the crab starts moving again."

"I can give it a shot, but wouldn't it just be better to pick up the crab and take it off the road, and…?"

"No, we can't do that," Ōno didn't let him finish. "Think about it. It would defeat the entire purpose of the boy and the dog getting this far. The boy is following his grandpa's last wish, going along with this crab to the sea. His grandpa must have thought that if the boy could do this, he'd become a man, that he'd be able to look after himself. That's what must be behind it. 'Self-reliance'—that's what he said, right? The crab doesn't care if you pick it up or not. But then the crab isn't really doing it itself. His grandpa wanted this kid to learn to be strong. That's why he wanted to show him that this crab could make the ten-kilometer journey over the mountains and fields to get to the sea on its own, don't you think?"

Kaida was silent.

"What'll happen if you touch that crab? Everything that kid has been through so far will go up in a puff of smoke."

"I see. Yeah, you're right."

"What difference is it really going to make in any of our lives if we end up waiting an hour or two?"

"All right, I'll do it." Kaida stood up energetically. "If anyone still insists on trying to drive through, I'll turn my truck sideways to block the road."

"We don't want any fights. Ask for their cooperation. We need cooperation." Ōno looked back at Shin'ichi Todai.

2

"…And so, everyone, what we need to do is just wait a little until the crab rests up and can go on its way again…" Kaida, wearing nothing but his boxers, was giving the speech of his life. He'd never spoken in public before. He never thought he could. But the darkness helped. Once he'd started talking, the words came to him in a way he'd never expected.

He'd finished explaining the circumstances. Now all he had to do was persuade everyone to cooperate.

"In other words, this crab has already traveled, under its own power, six kilometers, as the crow flies—probably seven or eight when you consider all the twists and turns and ups and downs. The sea is only four kilometers from here, in a straight line. The boy has spent four days getting this far, stopping when the crab stopped, walking when the crab walked. You've got to admit, that's something. His grandfather's dead. The boy buried his grandfather, and set out to follow the crab to the sea. He's setting out on his own new life. That's what his grandfather intended. Knowing he didn't have long to live, he decided to teach the boy to be independent, to be self-reliant, to become a man who could do whatever it took to survive. That's what I think. Both the grandfather and the boy were completely alone in the world. All they had was each other."

"You're good, Mr. Boxer Shorts!"

"I'm just an ordinary truck driver," replied Kaida to his heckler.

"You should run for the town council. You'd be elected hands down!"

"You've got to listen to me about this crab."

"If it was me, I'd fry it up as tempura and eat it!"

"Stop! You're breaking his heart!"

Several hecklers chimed in.

"Like I said, I'm just an ordinary truck driver. All I do is drive, day after day. I'm not handsome like Bunta the Trucker in the movies, and the women never go for me. I'm a complete washout. You, you all own your own cars...but I'm not here to talk about our differences. Something has brought us all together, stuck us here on this highway together. Can you all agree, and just wait until the crab moves out of the way? They way I see it, in all the years I've been driving I must have run over hundreds of crabs. They were all living things. Some of them might have traveled a long way to get to the sea and lay their eggs. Or they may have been bringing food to their offspring. When I think about that, I want to help this one crab out if I can. I'd like to ask you to take this as our shared karma, and let's just celebrate this crab's safe crossing of the highway."

"Well said, Naked Guy!"

"Thank you."

"You can be our chairman. Of the...'Association to Protect the Crab, the Boy, and the Dog.' We'll all be committee members. Let's wait until this crab gets going again. We'll wait till morning if we have to. After all, it's only one night. I've always wanted to do at least one good thing in my life. Let's help this crab. Of course, while we're talking, the crab may have already started moving. If so, this will be the shortest-lived protection association in world history. Hey, it'll be fun. If we had some *shōchū*, I'd propose a toast."

This was delivered by a middle-aged man.

Cheerful laughter arose from the crowd. In fact, there was a note of exhilaration in it—the exhilaration that came from recognizing a shared link among the people gathered there, and between them and one little crab, even if it meant closing a national highway. This feeling of togetherness, of solidarity, might well evaporate after a brief time. Or it might continue until the morning. An odd acquiescence to that possibility, a readiness to just go with the flow, seemed to pass through them all.

News of the event reached the Tateyama Police Department at 11:20 p.m. One of the cars caught in the traffic jam was equipped with a wireless radio. The driver had called in to the police and asked them to do something about it.

The problem seemed to be about ten kilometers outside Tateyama City. Officially it was under the jurisdiction of Maruyamamachi.

But, given the situation, officers from the Tateyama Police Department went to the scene.

Traffic Department Head Inspector Iwata took three patrol cars. Cars carrying reporters from the local Chiba television station and newspapers went along with them.

The crab wasn't moving.

It produced a froth of small bubbles. Its eye stalks remained extended. Usually it lowered its eyes and folded its legs when it slept. But the area was brightly lit. The crab was tired, but she couldn't go completely to sleep. Her alertness shone in her two eyes. She produced foam, then let it disappear. Kuro was laying in front of the crab. The shiba inu's nose was black. Wet and shiny, it looked like pure curiosity, distilled to a concentrated essence. A gap of about ten centimeters separated the nose and the crab. Kuro's eyes were focused on the crab.

Shin'ichi Todai was sitting with his knees up and his chin resting on them.

These three figures were surrounded by a large group of men.

Kaida, who had been appointed the chairman of the Association to Protect the Crab, the Boy, and the Dog, was sitting next to Kuro.

Aka's going to sleep—that's what Shin'ichi Todai said. The crab had slept three nights since leaving the foot of Mount Kompira. This was the fourth night. Because of the zig-zags in their route, they must have traveled seven or eight kilometers. That meant about two kilometers a day. The crab definitely looked tired, settling down to sleep, but still gripping the earth and producing a small amount of foam.

Shin'ichi Todai was also tired. His eyes, focused on the crab, occasionally closed. As Kaida watched the boy, he was overcome with an ineffable sense of embarrassment. The boy's face had that inviolable dignity, that untouched purity so characteristic of boys. There was no slackness or sagging anywhere to be seen. It seemed to possess infinite potential. It even seemed divine.

Crabs sleep at night. But they normally retire to a hole. Forced to sleep out in the open over the last several days, the crab seemed unsettled, and just when the boy thought she was asleep, she'd start moving again. The boy had basically not slept since they'd started. If he relaxed his watch, he drifted off to sleep. Then the crab would disappear. It was Kuro who prevented this. Whenever the crab started to move, the dog would bark and wake the boy.

That's how they'd gotten this far.

"Why not shut the crab up somewhere when you're sleeping, at least?" Kaida had asked. The boy shook his head. He'd promised his grandpa he wouldn't touch the crab. If he did, it meant that the crab hadn't reached the sea on its own.

The only thing he and the dog had done, he said, was to protect the crab from rats and crows and other enemies.

The rigor of the boy's commitment to his promise made Kaida feel ashamed. He asked himself if he'd been like that as a boy. No, he hadn't.

Both the boy and the dog were very peculiar, he thought. The boy was attached to the crab. Most boys who kept a crab didn't think they could communicate with it and wouldn't consider accompanying it on its journey to the sea to spawn. The dog was strange, too. People have the capacity to imagine they're communicating with a crab. Dogs don't. Yet this dog realized that it was the crab's protector and watched over it, keeping its nose within reach at all times.

The strange spell conjured by the combination of the boy's determination, the dog's curiosity, and the crab's instinct had cast its bewitchment over Kaida and the others.

And as a result the highway was closed.

Kaida wondered what kind of man this grandfather, who had raised the boy and the dog, had been. On his deathbed, he had assigned the boy and the dog a preposterous task.

Shin'ichi Todai could not hide the sadness on his face. There was a darkness in his dignified visage. Kaida thought it might the sadness he felt at losing his grandfather.

He heard the sound of a police car approaching.

It seemed to have stopped, and several police officers and reporters joined the group.

"Who's the ringleader?" asked Inspector Iwata, making his way through the crowd. He didn't know what was going on. The caller on the wireless had said that a crab was sleeping on the highway, and as a result, it was closed down. Iwata, of course, didn't believe this. But indeed, the highway was closed.

"Me," said Kaida, standing up. "I'm the chairman of the Association to Protect the Crab, the Boy, and the Dog. I guess."

"Stop the nonsense!" shouted Iwata. He thought he was being ridiculed. There was, to be sure, a crab sitting on the asphalt, blowing foam, between a boy and a dog. They were surrounded by forty or fifty men. That was the apparent situation, but there must be another explanation, something they were hiding. Otherwise they'd invented the whole thing just to make fools of the police.

Iwata was on his guard, determined not to be played for a fool.

"It's not nonsense."

"What's your name?"

"Masagoro Kaida. I'm thirty-four. I'm a truck driver."

"Show me your license."

"My license? It has nothing to do with that."

"I don't care what it has to do with, you all need to move your cars immediately. What do you think you're doing?" demanded Iwata roughly.

"We're the members of the Association to Protect the Crab, the Boy, and the Dog. We won't move our cars until the crab moves!" said one of the men in the circle.

"That's right! Don't give in, Chairman!"

The men started shouting. "Stand your ground! Don't let them touch the crab! If they do, we'll set the police cars on fire!"

"I'll arrest you all for violating the traffic laws," said Iwata, startled by the force of the reaction. The men's determination had the power of a surging wave.

A short, balding middle-aged man standing by Iwata spoke, his voice shaking with emotion, "Go ahead, arrest us. We're all complete strangers. Here on the highway we formed this Association to Protect the Crab, the Boy, and the Dog. We've been here two hours like this. Why do you think that is? Maybe we're just acting up, maybe it's a crazy whim. We don't care. When the crab moves, we'll all go our separate ways. That's all there is to it. It has nothing to do with the police. Get out of here."

"Call for backup," Iwata barked at one of his men.

The television cameras were rolling. The cameras of the newspaper reporters were flashing.

"Look here, officer," Ōno tried to mediate. "It's nothing big or important. Please hear us out. It's this crab. This crab is heading to the sea to spawn. They only spawn on the full and new moons from September through October. And only then from between about 7:30 and 9:00 p.m. This crab set out from a place called Aono at the foot of Mount Kompira on September 1. There're only two days left until the full moon on September 6. The sea is another four kilometers away. This is a crisis. It has to walk another four kilometers in just two days."

"Why's that a crisis?"

"Why? What do you…?"

"Someone can just take it there," said Iwata angrily.

"No, you see…" Ōno wiped the perspiration from his forehead. He continued to explain. With great eloquence, he explained everything the boy and the dog had gone through to accompany the crab this far.

"I see," said Iwata, relieved that there actually was something behind the incident. But at the same time, he was angered by the silliness of the entire thing. He couldn't believe that rational adults would do such a thing.

"What's your name?" he asked, crouching in front of the boy.

"Shin'ichi Todai." The boy looked at Iwata.

"Where are your parents?"

"I don't have any," replied the boy, shaking his head.

"You don't have any? Are they dead?"

"Noooo," said the boy, slowly shaking his head.

"Well then, what happened?"

"My mother left us. Then my father went away somewhere, too. Then, I wanted to see the ocean, so I went there. Kuro was on the beach. I was playing with Kuro and Grandpa came up. He asked me where I came from, so I said Tokyo. He asked me if I wanted to come to his house…"

"When was all this?"

"About two years ago."

The rising excitement of the reporters was palpable.

"Your grandpa lived in Aono?"

"He used to be a fisherman in Shirahamamachi, he said. But he's dead now…"

"Dead? When?"

"Two days before the crab started out." The boy was looking at the crab.

"And…"

"He said, 'When I die, bury my body in the flower bed and follow along after the crab. The crab's instinct will take her straight to the sea.' On the way, she could get hit by a car or attacked by an animal. Me and Kuro, we're supposed to protect her, he said. But he told me not to touch the crab. To let her get to the sea on her own. The crab's name is Aka. I caught her when I went to the beach with Grandpa, and I was keeping her as a pet." His eyes remained fixed on the crab.

"You buried your grandfather, then?"

"Yup," said the boy, nodding. "Grandpa grew marigolds and stocks. I dug a hole in the flower bed and Kuro and me buried him."

Iwata fell silent.

The reporters began talking excitedly to each other.

"Will you come to the police station with me? I want you to show me where you buried your grandpa."

"I can't," said the boy, looking at Iwata, shaking his head vigorously. "Without me and Kuro, Aka won't make it to the sea. Grandpa told me. He said Aka had over fifty thousand eggs. They'd all die."

"The police will take your crab to the sea. It'll be all right."

"No."

"I'm afraid you don't have any choice, Mr. Todai." Iwata took the boy by the arm.

"Officer," Kaida held down Iwata's arm. "You can't do that."

"Do you intend to put up resistance? This boy buried a body."

"All he did was follow his grandpa's last request." Kaida had gone pale.

"Do you want to be arrested?"

"You'll have to arrest me, too, then." The small middle-aged man who had spoken up earlier stepped forward. "On the way to spawning, the crab stopped on the highway. The boy and the dog are accompanying her. We're all trying to help them. That's all there is to it, isn't it? Why do you have to arrest anybody? If you're going to arrest him, you'll have to arrest all of us. Why are you getting your back up about it?"

"It's the law."

"This boy is nine years old. A nine-year-old boy follows his dear grandpa's last wish and buries him—where's that against the law? Where are your human feelings?"

The man's name was Yoshioka. He was a carpenter in Chiba City. He pressed up to Iwata with a menacing expression.

"The law is the law," Iwata blanched.

"Then the law can eat shit!" shouted Kaida. "The dead man isn't going anywhere. It's just two more days. Just four more kilometers to the ocean. This crab has to get to the sea by after seven on the night of the full moon. Otherwise it can't spawn. Why can't you wait two days? Why can't you go dig up the body yourself? Go ahead—just try to take this boy away. I won't sit by and let you, that's for sure."

"That's right! The whole association will fight you!" Cheers rose from the men.

"Take the boy away!" Iwata shouted to the officers with him.

"So you want a fight? Bring it on!" Kaida took off his flip-flops and held one up as if to strike with it. A highly charged emotion, bordering on menace, was stirring the men of the protection association.

"Now just hold on a minute." A white-haired man stepped out of the group. "My name is Hirose. I'm an attorney. Up until just recently, I was a public prosecutor at the Tokyo High Public Prosecutors Office."

"What does that have to do with anything?" asked Iwata, his voice shaking with rage.

"As a public prosecutor, I'd agree with how you want to handle the situation. But I'm not in that position any more. Given the situation, as someone said earlier, it might be better to just let things take their course. By morning, the crab will get off the highway. Till then, couldn't you be supportive of this feeling of community and togetherness that has naturally sprung up among a group of strangers because of a crab, a boy, and a dog?"

"But the body…" gasped Iwata.

"That's no big deal, either. I'm sure the law has the magnanimity to allow this boy two days of grace."

Iwata didn't reply.

"As a favor to a white-haired old man, can't you see your way to allow this, just this once?"

Iwata remained silent.

"Inspector Iwata," one of the reporters called out to him. "We members of the press agree with the gentleman. Couldn't you arrange it just this once with the police chief? To permit the boy and the dog to accompany the crab all the way to the sea? With your cooperation, I'm sure it could be arranged."

Iwata didn't answer.

The crab just kept blowing bubbles.

3

The crab was sleeping.

She fell asleep at 2:00 a.m. That was the time when all the lights around it were finally turned off.

She had stopped foaming and folded her legs, pulling in her eye stalks to sleep. The boy and the dog slept beside her.

The members of the Association to Protect the Crab, the Boy, and the Dog returned to their cars. Only Kaida and a few others, along with several of the reporters, remained by the boy.

Using his backpack as a pillow, Shin'ichi Todai was breathing lightly in his sleep.

An all-night program was playing on one of the car radios. The DJ repeated the story of the crab, the boy, and the dog. He talked excitedly, saying that people from all over the country were phoning in.

Kaida was listening. DJs have great sources. They get their traffic information not just from the police but from highway service islands throughout the country. They're always looking for something interesting to share with listeners. They were certainly quick to pick up on this story of the crab, the boy, and the dog.

Junior and senior high school students listen to all-night radio programs, too, while they're studying. So do people who drive for a living. Kaida enjoyed the all-night shows. Now he was in the news himself. He felt suddenly important. No, more than important; he felt as if from today on he'd never be the same. He felt he'd have to change.

The members of the protection association all had different jobs and professions. He wondered what it was that made such different men agree to spend a night together, completely out of the blue. He had no good explanation for it. At the same time, he couldn't help but feel a certain humanity, a warmth of fellow feeling.

He decided to stop driving carelessly. The men he was spending this night with were of all different sorts. Some of them were no doubt the kind who, once they were in their cars, would jostle for position on the road and curse out any other driver who got in their way. But, he realized, they were all the same inside. It was good to have this warm, friendly feeling about complete strangers.

The sky was filled with an enormous number of stars.

Kaida looked up at them.

The crab began to move before dawn.

The dog barked to let Shin'ichi Todai know.

The crab stood up, crawled quickly sideways, and left the highway. She was too quick for the news photographers to capture her with their cameras. It appeared as if the crab was looking for her chance to flee. A field started at the side of the highway. Beyond the field was a pine forest. The crab rushed into the field.

The dog followed her.

The boy rubbed his eyes, pulled on his backpack, and followed the dog.

Kaida ran to his truck. He blew the horn to wake everyone up. The crab has taken off, he shouted. Everyone came running.

The protection association members lined up along the edge of the highway. No one followed into the field. They'd promised not to. The rest was up to the crab, the boy, and the dog.

"Hang in there, sonny!" someone yelled. "See the crab all the way to the ocean. And let her give birth to her fifty thousand baby crabs."

The boy looked back. He bowed his head.

They all watched him head off. The crab was moving straight toward the sea. Three kilometers ahead, they'd run into the tracks for the Uchibō Line. When they'd crossed those, they still had to get over the Daini Flower Line that ran along the coast. Then they'd have less than a kilometer left. They'd reach the shore near Shirako.

But the crab was moving very slowly, not making much progress. The boy seemed to have stopped. The dog looked back at him from time to time from the high grass. The boy seemed to be putting his backpack down and taking some food out of it. He gave it to the dog. He ate too, as he walked.

"It's a long way," someone murmured. "Too long."

"No," said another. "The crab has already come six or seven kilometers. It's a short way, given its whole life. And for the boy, it's just a single moment of his life."

"Yes, but…" said another, "What could his parents have been thinking, abandoning him like that?"

No one had an answer.

Eventually, one by one, the men turned around.

Kaida went back to his truck.

Engines were roaring. The entire highway was filled with their sound. Kaida started driving. He drove past the young man who had almost picked a fight with him. He had the same pissed-off expression. The driver of the next car raised his arm in greeting. So did the next. They were all smiling.

As the cars passed each other, moving in opposite directions, the drivers all waved and smiled.

Eventually the traffic jam was transformed into two long lines of cars snaking off in either direction, out of sight.

Shin'ichi Todai stopped.

The sun had risen. He'd been walking for about three hours. A dead tree lay across the path. Aka was heading straight for it. He thought she'd try to walk around it, but she apparently decided to climb over it.

A large praying mantis stood atop the log. Its wings gleamed in the sunlight. Its big eyes were menacing.

"Wait, Kuro."

Kuro had seen the mantis and was about to chase it away. Shin'ichi stopped him. Aka hadn't noticed the mantis. She would run into it when she reached the top of the log. Shin'ichi didn't know which was stronger, the praying mantis or Aka. If they were going to fight, he thought, he'd let them. Denkichi Nagashino— Grandpa—had said he should accompany the crab to the sea with the least possible human interference.

He had to chase away large animals. But Shin'ichi didn't know if a praying mantis fit into that category.

Aka climbed up the fallen tree. When a crab extends its eyestalks, it can see all around. But Aka was walking through the tall grass and couldn't see into the distance. Aka had no idea that the praying mantis was waiting atop the log. As soon as she saw it, she walked right up to it. The mantis waved its forearms. Aka stopped. They looked at each other. The sharp blades of the mantis's forearms sparkled in the sun.

Kuro looked on, his nose quivering.

Aka made the first move. She approached the insect. The mantis rose to its full height and struck down with its forearms. It grabbed the crab's shell.

Aka's left claw was the large one. It moved slowly to enclose the praying mantis's thorax. The mantis struggled in her grasp. It spread its wings and tried to fly away. But Aka was clinging firmly to the dead wood of the log. The mantis struggled two or three times. Its thorax was cut in half by Aka's claw.

"Way to go, Aka!" murmured Shin'ichi, as he sat in the shade nearby.

Aka began to eat the mantis. She cut it up expertly with her smaller claw and put the pieces in her mouth. Her scarlet claws glittered in the sunlight. She looked like a warrior in shining red armor.

He had caught Aka at the end of July.

Shin'ichi and Kuro had gone with Denkichi in his beat-up truck to Shirahamamachi. While Denkichi was taking care of his business, Shin'ichi played with Kuro along the shoreline. Kuro discovered the red crab, which had taken refuge in a stone fence in a little dale near the shore. Shin'ichi stuck a stick into the hole. Aka grabbed the stick. When Shin'ichi pulled it out, the crab came with it, still powerfully grasping the stick. Another crab was in the hole. Shin'ichi captured it in the same way.

He showed Denkichi. What are you going to do with them, Denkichi asked. His brow seemed to cloud over. Shin'ichi said he wanted to keep them as pets. That's all right, then, Denkichi said.

On the drive home, Denkichi told Shin'ichi that they were red-clawed crabs. They mate from the end of July to August. After twelve or thirteen hours, the female lays eggs. She then attaches the eggs with a sticky membrane to her underside and keeps them there. At first the eggs are a pale lavender, but they gradually become whitish. She keeps them attached to her underside for twenty to thirty days.

On a night of either the full or new moon from September to October, the female crabs gather at the shore. They spawn from about 7:30 p.m. to 9:00 p.m. They wait for the tide to rise, and when the waves wash over them, they use their legs to release their eggs into the withdrawing waves. They do that several times, until all their eggs have been released into the sea.

Then the females return to their holes.

When Denkichi was a boy, there were huge numbers of crabs. On spawning night, sometimes tens of thousands of them would crowd onto the beach. Red-clawed crabs travel up rivers and valleys to places quite distant from the sea. They can spawn wherever there's water, in a river or a stream. The eggs flow down on the current into the sea. But most crabs go to the sea to spawn.

It was an amazing and impressive sight, Denkichi said.

Shin'ichi watched Denkichi's face in profile as he said all this. He'd heard that Denkichi was close to seventy years old. His hair was a mixture of white and black. His cheeks were deeply etched with vertical wrinkles that seemed carved into his skin, which was the color of the rocks along the seashore. His profile seemed very sad. Since he was speaking of his childhood, you'd have expected him to be talking in a happy, dreamy way, but that wasn't the case. Something clouded his thin face in profile. Only some time later did Shin'ichi find out what it was.

If you're going to take care of a living thing, said Denkichi, you have to take responsibility for it. Eventually the crab will lay eggs. A small crab might lay ten or twenty thousand; a large one fifty or sixty thousand. In an aquarium, the eggs will die. You'll have to return her to the sea. All living things have feelings. They have instincts. When the time comes for the crab to release her eggs, she'll set out for the sea. Her instincts will tell her what direction to go.

Shin'ichi promised to bring her back to the sea.

That would make the crab happy. There were roads along the coast now. Cement sea walls had been built. The roads were filled with cars. Crabs were run over and killed. Even if a few of the crabs succeeded in releasing their eggs, there was still no place for the baby crabs that hatched to live. There were no more stone walls, and if they tried to go up the rivers, they'd find them blocked by sluices. And now all the riverbanks were covered in poured concrete. Crabs were rapidly disappearing. It would be terrible if we made them extinct. As much as possible we should avoid killing living things.

That's what Denkichi said.

When he spoke about living things, his expression became stern.

Denkichi was usually smiling. He grew cut flowers to earn his living. He lived alone in a little farmhouse. He did his own cooking, washing, and flower cultivation. From spring through summer he grew marigolds and stocks. He had a little less than an acre of fields. He also grew a few sunflowers in the summer. His entire earnings for the year were about one million yen.

The only other income he had was about two hundred thousand yen in his old-age pension. That was everything.

Denkichi smiled and said it was enough to take care of Shin'ichi and Kuro.

Shin'ichi remembered his smile.

His brown face when he smiled seemed to smell of the sea.

Since going to live with Denkichi, Shin'ichi had stopped going to school. Aono was deep in the mountains, too far away from the elementary school. And he didn't want to go to school. His mother had run off with a younger man three years earlier. It drove his father to madness. His father was a taxi driver, a serious, hardworking man. After his wife left, he started drinking heavily, gambling, destroying himself. In the end he seemed to lose his mind and then, one day, he just left home and didn't come back.

Shin'ichi's uncle—his father's brother—took him in. There were two children in the family. It was a small house. Shin'ichi felt very uncomfortable there. That didn't surprise him, but the difference in the way his aunt and uncle treated him and the way they treated their own children was even starker than he'd expected. Shin'ichi had just started elementary school when his father disappeared. That school was too far from his uncle's house, and Shin'ichi didn't feel like going to another school.

He bought a train ticket with his allowance money. He wanted to go to the sea. After he saw the sea, he was going to commit suicide.

Denkichi picked him up. Denkichi asked him about his situation, and then contacted his uncle. If you want the boy, he's yours, his uncle said. Shin'ichi began living with Denkichi, and school wasn't a problem any more. When Shin'ichi said he didn't want to go, Denkichi said okay. Denkichi got some textbooks from an elementary school somewhere. He told Shin'ichi to at least learn to read and write. That would be enough for now, he said. Other subjects, he said, you could study them when you felt like it.

He was a nice man.

With tears in his eyes, Shin'ichi looked for Denkichi's face in the clear sky above.

Something cast a shadow over the sky, like an arrow cutting sideways across his field of vision.

Before Shin'ichi could stand up, Kuro, who had been at his side, rushed out. A bird of prey like a buzzard was about to attack Aka as she stood atop the fallen tree. The bird's body hovered over Aka. At the same instant, Kuro leaped out and threw himself against the bird's body. The bird let out a short screech. Kuro and the bird were tangling with each other in the air. They immediately fell to the ground. Kuro had the bird pinned, its black wings spread out on the grass.

Shin'ichi came running. Aka was no longer on the fallen tree. Shin'ichi looked around. Aka was nowhere to be seen. *Maybe the bird had already swallowed her*, Shin'ichi thought. His legs trembled. He didn't want to step on Aka, so he couldn't just walk around heedlessly.

"Kuro!"

Kuro had the bird in his jaws and was shaking it. Its feathers went flying, flashing in the sunlight.

"Kuro! Aka's gone!" shouted Shin'ichi, in tears.

4

Shin'ichi and Kuro sat crouched in the shade.

Aka was gone. Shin'ichi had crawled carefully around the entire area looking for her. On hands and knees, he gradually expanded the circle he was investigating. Kuro looked, too. He searched the area, parting every blade of grass, but no Aka.

Kuro searched desperately. He pressed his nose to the ground, looking for the scent. Shin'ichi placed his hopes on Kuro's sense of smell. They had lost track of Aka several times before. Aka would walk off while Shin'ichi and Kuro were sleeping. But each time, Kuro would press his nose to the ground, catch a scent, and rush off in one direction. He'd immediately find Aka, both her eye stalks up, walking along in alert mode.

But observing Kuro, Shin'ichi despaired. After sniffing around the area, wagging his tail, he started following Aka's trail back toward the highway. That was proof that he hadn't been able to catch her fresh scent.

The bird must have eaten her. It had been flying up from the fallen tree. That had been the moment it had eaten Aka.

Shin'ichi didn't know what kind of bird it was. *Maybe it was a buzzard*, he thought. Last winter, he saw a flock of them roosting in the woods. Denkichi had told him they were related to eagles and hawks and were called gray-faced buzzards. They were migrating south, he said. This bird looked like those. It was about the size of a crow, with four bands on its tail feathers.

Now that buzzard had been torn apart by Kuro and was laying there like a limp rag. Its feathers were scattered all about and its body covered with blood. If he cut open its belly, maybe he'd find Aka—thought Shin'ichi, but he couldn't bring himself to do that. Aka would already be dead anyway. Gray-faced buzzards ate snakes, frogs, and insects. It could kill something the size of a red-clawed crab with a single strike of its sharp beak. And then it ate her. Her shell must have been torn apart and her insides ripped out.

Shin'ichi didn't feel like opening up the bird to see that.

Kuro was lying down, looking blankly at the grass shining in the sunlight.

Stroking the dog's head, Shin'ichi looked at its black eyes. They seemed to be crying. Kuro seemed sad that his friend had been eaten.

He was a strange dog. He tried to befriend all sorts of small animals. Even lizards and snakes. Even a praying mantis. But none of them responded. Kuro tried very hard to befriend the two crabs Shin'ichi had taken from the seashore. When Shin'ichi let the crabs out in his room, Kuro would spend hours playing with them. The crabs raised their claws to threaten him, but eventually Kuro's persistence wore them down. They learned to eat right in front of the resting Kuro, and when Kuro was eating they would climb up into his bowl.

Now one of those crabs had been eaten by a gray-faced buzzard.

"Should we go home, then, Kuro?" said Shin'ichi to the dog. He looked up into the sky, his eyes dry now. But when he went home,

Denkichi wouldn't be there. Just before he died, Denkichi told him that he had written out a will. He said he had left the land and the house to Shin'ichi. He asked Shin'ichi to take care of Kuro, and then he drew his last breath.

Shin'ichi had no idea what he would do if he went back home.

"No, Kuro. Let's go to the sea. Aka may not be alive, but all her kind will be there. Tomorrow night is the full moon. Lots of red-clawed crabs will be there releasing their eggs. We'll go home after we see that."

The scene that Denkichi had described for him remained vivid in his mind. The red-clawed crabs would come from everywhere, waving their claws as they rushed to the shore. The beach would be blanketed with tens of thousands of crabs. When they had released their eggs, the color of the sea was changed by the eggs floating on its surface. He wanted to see that. Aka wouldn't be there. Aka had been eaten by the gray-faced buzzard. What a pitiful end, after spending four days walking all that way.

He should have carried her.

He regretted that. If he had disobeyed Denkichi's instructions and carried her to the sea in a cage, Aka would be safe. She'd have been able to join the other crabs and release her fifty thousand eggs into the sea. Shin'ichi resented Denkichi's insistence that he let the crab walk to the sea on her own, his insistence that living things shouldn't be interfered with.

He wanted to see the others of her kind, the other red-clawed crabs. Things were different from the way they'd been when Denkichi was a boy. There probably weren't great droves of crabs now. Maybe there'd only be two or three. Or maybe none at all. Maybe they'd all been run over by cars, eaten by gray-faced buzzards and kites and crows. Maybe the bright light of the full moon would fall on nothing but the sound of the waves.

If Aka had arrived safely to the shore, she might have been the only crab releasing her eggs that night.

Even so, Shin'ichi decided he wanted to see the sea on the night of the full moon when Aka should have been releasing her eggs.

"Let's go, Kuro."

Shin'ichi put on his backpack.

Kuro stood. Just as he was about to start walking, his black nose went up in the air. He raised it up to the sky and began to sniff, his nose aimed at the trunk of a tree. There it stopped.

"Aka!"

The blood drained from Shin'ichi's veins and then quickly poured back in.

Aka was climbing down the trunk of the tree. She was blowing foamy bubbles. Kuro barked. Shin'ichi approached her. It was Aka, without a doubt. She reached Shin'ichi's eye level. Shin'ichi reached out his hand and then stopped. Denkichi's voice echoed in his mind.

"Your leg..." said Shin'ichi softly. One of Aka's left front legs was missing. Aka seemed to be foaming because she was hurt.

Aka climbed down the tree trunk. Kuro touched the crab with his nose and wagged his tail. Aka began to walk. She made no mistake of her direction, She was headed toward the sea.

She may have been grabbed by the gray-faced buzzard, or maybe she had grabbed on to it somewhere with a claw, and then was shaken off, Shin'ichi realized. She was tossed up into the sky and landed on the tree.

In the sunlight Shin'ichi's face glowed the color of blood.

The story of the crab, the boy, and the dog had spread throughout Japan by noon that day.

The response to the all-night radio broadcast was enormous. The station was flooded with more calls than its switchboard could handle. The overflow was so extreme it blew some of the station's fuses.

The television morning shows picked up the ball from there. The footage taken by the CHIBA TV crew was sent to every station in the country, and the photos taken by the local journalists were everywhere.

You could see everything from the confrontation between the Association to Protect the Crab, the Boy, and the Dog and the police, to the crab sitting on the highway foaming at the mouth, to the boy and the dog crouched nearby watching over it.

Professor Tazawa of the Tokyo University Ocean Research Institute, an authority in crustaceology, was invited to appear on the morning shows and lecture on the red-clawed crab.

The regular news picked up the story after that. The nine o'clock news announced the exhumation of the body of Denkichi Nagashino that the boy Shin'ichi Todai had buried in his flower beds. The police searched the house and found Nagashino's will. It left everything to the boy and his dog, Kuro. It was clear from the wording of the will that Nagashino knew his death was approaching.

The body was taken to a police laboratory for an autopsy.

The ten o'clock news announced Nagashino's cause of death. Tateyama Municipal Hospital had contacted the police with a report from the physician who had been treating Nagashino for the past year for lung cancer. It was a silent-phase cancer that caused the patient no pain. The doctor confirmed that Nagashino had reached the end of his natural life.

At the same time, the story of Shin'ichi Todai's life had been uncovered.

The newscaster announced with some hesitation that the boy was an orphan who had been abandoned by both of his parents.

The noon news contained film taken from a helicopter. It showed the boy and the dog walking under the bright sun. They had arrived at a settlement called Anbaya, a short distance south of the national highway. About one kilometer west of there, the boy and the dog turned south. Of course the cameras didn't pick up the crab. The sea was a little more than three kilometers away.

The full moon was September 6. In other words, tomorrow night. It was also the spring tide, and high tide would be at eight o'clock.

The newscaster asked Professor Tazawa whether the boy and the red-clawed crab could reach the sea by tomorrow night.

"I really couldn't say." Tazawa was about fifty and had a genial face.

A map of southern Chiba was hanging in the studio. Tazawa looked at it and replied, "There are two other crabs that are very similar to the red-clawed crab, live in the same environment, and have much the same behavior and life-patterns: the Benkei crab and the black Benkei crab. We can only guess how fast they walk.

We know how fast they are at short distances, but how far they could travel in a day…" Tazawa smiled.

"Maybe one, two, or three kilometers. We know that spiny lobsters, for example, can travel six kilometers in one night under water. Considering how long it's taken this red-clawed crab to get this far, I'd say about two kilometers a day is what you might expect. Based on that, it's not impossible that the crab will arrive at the seashore by tomorrow night."

"The crab left from the foothills of Mount Kompira on September 1. Could this be because it instinctively knew how long it would take to traverse the distance to the sea and arrive in time?"

"I can't answer that. Normally, I would say that's impossible. For example, some red-clawed crabs live at an altitude of two hundred meters. The crab larvae swim up the rivers and streams, become baby crabs, and gradually split off into smaller and smaller streams, rivulets, and wetlands, dispersing as they go. As long as they can follow wetlands, they can travel some distance. It's conceivable that those crabs travel several kilometers to return to the river or some other flowing water. They have a memory of having made the trip in the first place. They may even have a memory of how long it takes to make the journey. But for a red-clawed crab that has been artificially removed from its environment to realize that it is almost ten kilometers from the sea and be able to calculate how long it will take to return to the sea, and know which direction it should travel—well, that's something we never even imagined."

"But in fact that's just what this crab, boy, and dog are doing, isn't it?"

"I have to take my hat off to them."

"What do you think about the boy?"

"If he succeeds, it will be a wonderful thing. I hope he'll study marine biology when he gets older. I think the man who directed the boy to do this was right. This one little crab has made a journey of seven or eight kilometers. I'm sure it was very difficult. The old man wanted to give the boy something better than a school education—an education in life. If the boy is successful, he'll be the stronger for it. A red-clawed crab has to be in the water from about seven to eight o'clock in the morning and again at about four to five o'clock in the evening. That's when they're most vulnerable to their natural enemies. I wonder how the boy is dealing with that? It's no easy thing to see that crab all the way to the sea without ever touching it or interfering with it."

The smile disappeared from Tazawa's face.

The news made a big splash.

The evening papers that night were filled with photos of the crab, the boy, and the dog.

People were excited by the fact that a single crab had closed a national highway for five hours. They were moved and delighted to learn that a group of strangers had formed an Association to Protect the Crab, the Boy, and the Dog, had refused to be put off by warnings from the police, and had won the right for the crab to sleep.

Both the TV and the newspapers reported that officials at all levels were calling for everyone to leave the crab, the boy, and the dog alone. They sternly warned against people rushing to the scene to disturb their progress.

The TV stations and papers were flooded with telephone calls that day.

5

They were beside a small pond.

Aka was hiding beneath a rock. Dusk was falling. Shin'ichi and Kuro had just finished eating. They had a small campfire. A large tree root was burning. In the light of the flames, they could see Aka.

Aka was resting in a small indentation on the underside of the stone. Her legs were folded up and she was crouched flat. She had just finished eating a dried sardine soaked in water. Her eye stalks were retracted.

Shin'ichi wondered what she was thinking. He didn't know whether crabs even thought at all. Aka had departed from the foothills of Mount Kompira and headed straight south. She must have been thinking of the sea. She must have been thinking of the others of her kind.

To Shin'ichi, she was such a little thing—a small creature completely enclosed in her shell. What part of her did she think with?

"If we don't move faster tomorrow, we won't make it to the seashore by evening, Aka," said Shin'ichi. He had brought a map. Below the national highway was a settlement called Anbaya. There were two ponds to the left of it. Aka walked down where you could see the ponds. Based on that, he estimated they had traversed about half the distance from the highway to the sea.

Aka had lost a leg, but it didn't seem to have made much difference in her speed. She seemed fine. On the way she encountered grasshoppers and other insects several times. On each occasion, Aka chased after them, waving her big claw. If she could do that, she must be fine, Shin'ichi concluded.

Shin'ichi believed that Aka would arrive at the shore in time. She had fifty thousand eggs on the bottom of her shell. If she didn't get to the sea, those eggs would all die. Aka must have known that she would make it.

Denkichi said she should arrive at the sea at high tide on the night of the full moon.

Denkichi knew a lot about all kinds of living things. He told Shin'ichi stories about many different creatures. There was something sad about his tales of plants and animals.

Once Shin'ichi had a question for Denkichi, who always said that you shouldn't kill living things. If that was so, Shin'ichi said, he didn't understand why Denkichi had been a fisherman.

Denkichi didn't reply at the time.

His answer came one night about ten days before he died.

Denkichi was drinking *shōchū* at the time. He spoke while he drank, a little at a time.

Denkichi had a daughter. Her name was Chiyoko. When she was seven years old, she drowned in the ocean. That was the end of it. They never found her body.

There's a cape called Nojimazaki at Shirahamamachi. A lighthouse stands on the cape. Chiyoko was taken to the seashore by her elementary school teacher. It was a sunny day. The waves were gentle. The teacher was an expert swimmer. He never let the children out of his sight.

By the time he noticed the change in the ocean, it was too late. A huge wave swelled up in the water off the beach. The teacher screamed out to the children. Suddenly the giant black breaker smashed down, tearing at the children as they tried to flee.

The wave engulfed the children. They looked like scattering flower petals. The teacher was swallowed by the wave, too. Still, he tried desperately to save the kids. Several fishermen who had been on the shore went running into the water.

It was just the one giant wave.

Chiyoko was the only child they never found. The teacher and the fishermen kept on swimming and diving, looking for her. But she had simply vanished. One of the fishermen saw something strange. One place in the sea seemed to have risen and be moving. The fisherman went pale with fear.

It was the dorsal fin of a giant fish. The black dorsal fin quickly disappeared.

Denkichi was at home. When he received the news, he rushed to the shore and leaped into the water, without saying a word. He dived. He kept on diving. By that time a lot of fishing boats were in the water. So were a lot of fishermen. The fishermen cast out their nets. Professional abalone-diving women helped. The search continued in earnest until night, but Chiyoko's body wasn't found.

Several days later the search was called off.

After it had been canceled, Denkichi heard about the giant fish from the fisherman who had seen it.

Denkichi just nodded. He couldn't speak. Neither could Chiyoko's mother, Yayoi.

Several months later Yayoi left Denkichi.

Denkichi began to fish. A rumor arose that Chiyoko had been eaten by a giant grouper, and then it faded. Denkichi seemed to have no interest in the rumor. Denkichi's profession was pole-and-line fishing. He just went on fishing. People felt sorry for him, but no one approached the now somber Denkichi. He had always been a quiet type. After Chiyoko disappeared into the ocean, he closed up like a clam.

A year later, Denkichi suddenly stopped fishing with a pole. He anchored his boat offshore and began diving. People regarded this new behavior with bewilderment. You can catch fish by diving, too. You spear them. Denkichi began bringing the fish he caught to the fisherman's association. Almost all of them were from the grouper family. Groupers can grow to an enormous size. There are records of fish weighing as much as 210 pounds being caught. They're tasty, too, so they fetch a good price.

But he didn't catch that many.

Even so, he continued diving.

Denkichi was looking for the giant grouper. He was looking for the giant grouper the fisherman had seen when the huge wave swept Chiyoko under. The giant grouper lives in rocky coastal waters. It can get so big as to be mistaken for a whale. There are records of giant groupers weighing well over half a ton. Ordinary fishing equipment is no match for such a fish. You use a harpoon. The harpoon is weighted with lead, and you plunge it into the giant grouper's back. There's a rope attached to the harpoon. The giant grouper begins to swim. Pulled by the fish, the boat speeds ahead like an arrow. You wait for the fish to tire, and then drag it back to the harbor.

But people only catch a giant grouper of that size perhaps once in a decade. If you find one, you can catch it, but finding one is quite a rare stroke of luck.

Denkichi was diving and searching for one. They didn't have scuba gear in those days. You used to hold a large rock to carry you down quickly. You got used to the depth gradually. After a year, you could easily handle depths of ten or eleven fathoms.

At first Denkichi didn't think that a giant grouper had swallowed Chiyoko. Giant groupers are not aggressive. They don't attack people. A half-ton giant grouper certainly could swallow a human being. Their mouths are as wide as a man is tall. But they have never been known to actively hunt humans.

That's what he'd always thought. But as time passed, for some reason the suspicion that a giant grouper had done this sprouted and grew in his mind. While he still doubted that a giant grouper had swallowed Chiyoko, in contradiction to his rational thoughts, a hatred began to grow inside him. He began to tell himself that a grouper *had* swallowed his daughter. Otherwise, what possible explanation was there for the disappearance of her body?

Abandoned by his wife, having lost his daughter, Denkichi nursed this feeling of loss as he fished. His sadness seemed to gnaw at him. He even thought that he wanted to die. If he could have joined his dead Chiyoko, he would have. He wanted to take care of her. His enmity for the giant grouper grew out of that feeling.

Denkichi kept diving for almost two years.

He discovered a giant fish. He found it in a rock cave. The cave was about five fathoms down. As Denkichi swam past the cavern, he sensed a subtle shift of the current. In front of the cave, at first waves seemed to push him away. Then he seemed drawn in. Startled, he looked more closely. The mouth of a huge fish filled the entire cavern opening.

Denkichi plunged his harpoon in with all his might. He jabbed it in with enough force to carry him inside the gaping mouth. The sharp harpoon disappeared into the huge mouth, with no feeling of having struck anything.

Denkichi was blown away by the force of the water expelled from the mouth of the enormous fish. Following the rope attached to the end of the harpoon, Denkichi floated upward. He hurried, but he wasn't fast enough. The giant fish began to swim. The rope was as tense as a steel cable. The boat was being pulled at astonishing speed. Denkichi was being pulled along with it. The force of the water threatened to dislodge his hands from the rope. He wrapped his legs around it and crawled slowly upward.

The boat skimmed over the surface of the sea like a speeding arrow.

He somehow managed to pull himself into the boat. He had swallowed a great deal of water. He had barely enough energy left to move. He lay there in a daze. The boat continued to run over the water. It was headed out to sea. The giant grouper was swimming with all its might. It kept going and going, out to sea.

The giant grouper only ran out of steam after an hour.

Denkichi began to try to bring it in. He pulled a little, then rested. It took several hours to bring it up to the side of the boat. When he did, Denkichi was astonished at its size. It was bigger than he had imagined. It was like a small whale.

When he started to direct the boat back to the harbor, he received a shock. The giant fish was now two fish. Next to the dead giant grouper, a slightly smaller one had somehow appeared when he wasn't looking.

It must have been the mate of the first one.

Looking down at the fish, Denkichi froze. A fishing boat is a very dangerous object to a fish. Knowing that full well, the dead grouper's mate had come to lay next to it.

After looking at the fish for a long time, Denkichi began to scull back to the harbor. The boat proceeded very slowly. The mate of the dead giant grouper remained by its side.

As Denkichi sculled, the sun set.

Denkichi lit a gas lamp. In its light, he could see the dorsal fins of the two groupers as the waves were hitting them. Their bodies seemed to dissolve into the sea's blackness.

It was the middle of the night before he neared the harbor. Just as before, there were two giant groupers alongside his boat.

Denkichi stopped sculling.

He cut the rope attached to the giant grouper. There was a wave, illuminated by the light of the gas lamp. It shone upon innumerable scales. The dead body of the first fish slowly sank. Like ghostly apparitions, the two giant fish descended silently into a world of darkness.

For some time after the fish had disappeared, Denkichi sat without moving, gazing over the side of his boat at the sea.

Denkichi abandoned the sea the next day.

He was in his mid-thirties.

Denkichi cleared some land at the foot of Mount Kompira and took up living there.

Nearly forty years had passed since then.

Then Denkichi died, watched over by Shin'ichi and Kuro.

When Shin'ichi heard this story from Denkichi, he cried. Denkichi related it all to him in his hoarse voice, searching for the words he needed. There were parts of the story Shin'ichi didn't understand. Denkichi's husky voice, like the sound of the wind over the waves, made up for that.

Denkichi continued. I don't have much longer. I'm going to die soon. That crab's belly is filled with eggs. Eventually, when the moment comes, she will go to the sea. I probably won't still be alive when that time comes. When the crab leaves, you and Kuro accompany her to the sea. If you don't, the crab will be eaten by some enemy or run over. But other than protecting her, you mustn't help the crab. She has to reach the sea through her own power. When parents are weak, their offspring are weak. Weak crabs will be born. That mustn't happen. The same is true for you. Your parents were both weak. You've inherited their tendencies. You have to get rid of them. That's another reason you need to lead the crab to the sea. If you reach the sea, you'll be a man. You'll be a fine, strong young man.

Denkichi's eyes sparkled as he said this. In the firelight, Shin'ichi saw them peering out from his deeply wrinkled face.

The night got darker and the flames grew redder. Shin'ichi looked at the crab. For a moment, he froze. Aka was in the indentation under the rock, her body pressed down, her claws raised. A frighteningly heavy-bodied viper was advancing toward her. Its showy pattern of brown blotches was picked up by the firelight.

Without even thinking, Shin'ichi stuck his hand into the indentation. He grabbed the snake, not knowing where, and pulled it out. As he was about to throw it aside, he felt a slight sting on his left thigh.

"Kuro! Come! Kuro!" He called. The dog had wandered off somewhere, but he returned immediately.

"Kill it! Kuro! Be careful!" He looked at Aka. Aka was in the same place. She still had her claws raised. Her eyes on her raised eye stalks sparkled in the firelight.

Kuro began to fight with the snake.

6

Shin'ichi Todai leaned against the rock.

He had a fever.

His left thigh, where the viper had bitten him, was purple and swollen.

About ten centimeters above his knee, there was a small bite mark, and it was bleeding. Shin'ichi had used his belt as a tourniquet on his thigh. He pulled it tight and pressed a knife to the bite. He closed his eyes and cut. He let the blood flow until it stopped.

Denkichi had taught him to do this. There were a lot of vipers around Denkichi's house. He'd told Shin'ichi to do this if he were bitten.

Kuro was looking apprehensively at Shin'ichi.

"Don't worry, Kuro. I won't die."

Shin'ichi stroked Kuro's head. His hand felt heavy, as did his entire body. He was shivering. His left thigh was throbbing in pain.

The fire had died down.

Shin'ichi looked at it. He didn't know if he could walk. If the swelling went down by morning, he thought he would be okay. But it might not. What would he do if he couldn't walk, he wondered. Aka would start out when morning came. If she didn't, she'd never reach the sea by the full tide tomorrow night. The crabs would release their eggs from about seven-thirty to nine at night. If Aka went off alone, she was sure to be killed. Enemies were waiting for her, and even more important, she still had to cross a prefectural highway.

Shin'ichi didn't know much about the viper's poison. He'd heard that it could kill you, depending upon where it bit you. Denkichi had told him that it was especially dangerous for old people and children.

Maybe I'll die.

He didn't want to die. What would Kuro do if he died? Kuro wouldn't know what to do.

In the darkness, the silence seemed to weigh down heavily.

Shin'ichi closed his eyes.

The fever seemed to be trying to carry his body away somewhere. Something like a heavy sleep descended over him. Would no one come to help him? he thought. But Denkichi was dead. Shin'ichi had no one other then Denkichi to turn to.

Thoughts of his parents rose dimly in his mind.

He didn't want to remember them. They were both like beasts. His mother, especially, was worthless. He had no memory of being loved, like other children did. She worked in a bar, and she smelled overpoweringly of cheap cosmetics. She was always running down his father. It had been that way from as far back as he could remember. They argued frequently.

After his mother ran off, his father changed. He was drunk all the time. He'd get plastered and curse his wife. He had a terrible mouth. He earned his living as a taxi driver. One night he had picked up a woman who seemed to be a little over twenty. She was drunk. After sending him on a long drive, she told him she had no money. She said she'd pay her fare with her body. His father had sex with her in the car. She said she didn't have anywhere to go, so his father brought the woman back to his apartment. She stayed on there.

That woman became Shin'ichi's mother.

"That slut, she spread her legs right there in the car"—that's what his father said. "That slut, she'd fuck anything." He called her every name in the book. "That slut, she's not your mother. Her cunt is like a public toilet."

Shin'ichi remembered all this. His parents were disgusting. He didn't miss either of them one bit. He had no wish to return to either of them, even if they came to get him. Why did he have to be born to such a father and a mother? His father telling him how he'd been conceived was especially painful. "Your mother spread her legs in the back seat of a taxi. That's how you were made—" that had hurt. It even made him feel like killing himself.

Shin'ichi shook these thoughts of his father and his mother out of his mind.

He tried opening his eyes a crack. Kuro was sleeping next to the dying campfire. He was lying there, looking at Shin'ichi. His black eyes were shining.

Shin'ichi woke to Kuro's growling.

It seemed to be near dawn. The fire was out. Kuro's growling was coming from somewhere ahead. It was a very threatening growl. Shin'ichi grabbed the flashlight, calling, "Kuro!"

The gleaming eyes of animals were visible in the flashlight's beam. Kuro was facing them. It seemed to be a group of stray dogs. He saw four of them.

"No, Kuro! Go back! Kuro!"

Leaning against the rock, Shin'ichi dragged himself up. At that moment Kuro's growl changed into an angry howl. In the light of the flashlight, several animals were going at each other. Angry howls filled the air.

He'll be killed!

Shin'ichi tried to run to the scene. But his left leg was useless. He fell. He crawled on both hands and his right knee. Kuro was being held down and bitten. Two dogs came toward Shin'ichi. They howled and bared their fangs. Shin'ichi had the tree root that had been burning in their campfire in his hand. He threw it at the two dogs coming at him. It was covered with ash, but beneath the ash coating it was still burning. It broke and flew in their direction. The two stray dogs let out yelps and fled.

So did the two who were fighting with Kuro.

"Kuro!"

Kuro was on the ground. Shouting, Shin'ichi approached. Kuro, however, immediately righted himself. Both his ears were torn. His left front leg also seemed to have been bitten, and the foot was twisted. Still, he wagged his tail.

"Good job, Kuro."

Shin'ichi hugged Kuro. Kuro was a shiba inu, so he was small. He had held off the four much larger stray dogs and fought with the spirit of a champion. Hugging Kuro, Shin'ichi wept.

Gradually the sky began to grow light.

Aka crawled out from beneath the stone. She approached the campfire. Her raised eyes glittered as if wet with dew. Kuro pushed his nose up to her and she responded by lifting her claws slightly. As if cautiously surveying the enemy territory, she looked around her and slowly started walking.

Shin'ichi put on his backpack. He could only use his right leg. His left thigh was terribly swollen. He tried hopping with one leg. A sharp pain shot through him. He gave up hopping and crawled. There was a group of trees a short distance away. He crawled to it.

Picking up a dead branch, he carved it with his knife and made a crutch. He wrapped the part that went under his arm with a cloth. It took him thirty minutes to fashion this. With the crutch under his left arm, he started walking. Kuro was following Aka. He was about a hundred meters ahead, walking and wagging his tail.

His left leg throbbed heavily. He had no feeling in it. Nothing but pain, and a heaviness, as if his leg was made of lead. Even with the crutch, walking was difficult. He had to rest after each step.

By the time he caught up with Kuro he was drenched with perspiration. Beneath the perspiration he was shivering. He sat down on a rock. Aka walked slowly past him.

The morning sun illuminated the grass. Birds that looked like kites were circling overhead.

"Stay with her, Kuro."

Kuro walked past, wagging his tail, both his ears crusted with dried blood. Shin'ichi's voice as he called to the dog was rough and listless, as if the life was draining out of it. Maybe he'd die. He knew that the poison had spread throughout his body. His breath was starting to smell bad. The fever was making him shiver uncontrollably.

"Grandpa." Shin'ichi called out for Denkichi. He saw Denkichi's face. His deeply wrinkled face, the color of a rock on the beach, was watching Shin'ichi. Help me, Grandpa, called out Shin'ichi.

Shin'ichi finally stood up. Kuro had stopped and was looking back at Shin'ichi. Shin'ichi started walking. He left the backpack on the stone. It contained his food. There was medicine in it, too. And the map. Bandages, socks, a shirt, and pants. He didn't want to leave it. But he didn't have the strength to carry it any more. Lowering his gaze to the level of the grass, he walked. His tennis shoes were covered with mud. The left leg of his jeans was cut off at the crotch. His thin leg was trembling. His leg had been strong enough to beat Kuro in a race. Now it hung there like a dead thing.

He was beset by an attack of dizziness. Whether standing or resting, he felt as if he were tipping over. *I don't have long*, he thought. The fever had fogged his mind. He seemed to see a little girl. He didn't know who it was. She seemed very neat and clean. Then he knew her name. It was Chiyoko.

Chiyoko was standing there in the grass, looking at Shin'ichi.

Masagoro Kaida parked his truck alongside the highway a little before 8:00 a.m.

He got out, carrying a bundle wrapped in a *furoshiki* cloth. He looked around, and ran quickly into the grass. Kaida ran and ran and ran. The bundle contained top-grade sushi and some packaged ham. It was food for the boy and the dog.

The television news was filled with the story yesterday. Kaida was in every report. It was always the same footage, him in his boxers, arguing with the police. He had been named as the chairman of the group that had spontaneously formed to protect the boy. His mother called him that night. She yelled at him for being on TV in his underwear. For the shame he'd caused her. But then she added, Wasn't letting the boy go off alone a good deed half done?

The TV, radio, and newspapers—all the news media—were urging people to leave the crab, the boy, and the dog alone. Otherwise all sorts of curiosity seekers would get in their way and make it into some kind of circus. Now that he was known as "the Chairman," if he got caught following the boy people would think he was trying to cash in on the event.

He kept on running for all he was worth.

He ran through the field and a patch of woods, and then he came across the remains of a campfire. Kaida's brow darkened. He found one leg of a pair of jeans, covered with blood. A dead viper was lying nearby. It was clear what had happened.

He ran farther and passed through the woods.

He heard a dog howling. He ran toward the sound.

In the midst of the grass under the blazing sun the boy lay collapsed in a heap. The dog was by his side, howling sadly.

Kaida picked up the boy. He was alive. He looked at Kaida with vacant eyes. The boy's body was hot in his arms.

"Don't worry. It's me, the Chairman of the Association to protect you. I'm taking you to the hospital."

"Aka...Aka..." murmured the boy.

"What happened to the crab?" Kaida asked the dog.

The dog ran straight ahead. Laying the boy down again, Kaida ran. After about three hundred meters, the dog stopped. Kaida looked down. The crab, seeing Kaida, lifted her claws. She was a large red crab.

"You stay with the crab," said Kaida to the dog. Kaida ran into the trees. He cut a vine, returned, and used the vine to tie the boy to his back.

"Aka...I have to follow Aka..." whispered the boy, his mouth to Kaida's ear.

"First we have to get you to a hospital."

"No—No. I promised Grandpa. Put...me down."

"You'll die if you don't get to the hospital."

"I don't...care. Put me...down."

The boy grabbed Kaida's hair.

Kaida didn't know what to do. He stood there and wiped his forehead with his hand. The dog came back.

"Hey, stupid dog! What are you doing!" Kaida shouted. Two or three crows flew up from the area where the crab had been. When he saw that, Kuro dashed straight toward them. Kaida did, too.

"All right, I suppose I have no choice. Don't blame me if you die," shouted Kaida, still running.

7

The helicopter arrived about thirty minutes later.

Kaida put the boy down. He mimed his need for help.

He ran up to the helicopter that had landed in the grass.

"You've got to bring a doctor. The boy was bitten by a viper."

"Who are you?"

The helicopter had been chartered by CHIBA TV.

"I just happened to be passing by."

"Wouldn't it be better to take the boy to the hospital?"

"He says he won't leave the crab, even if he dies."

"All right. I'll get a doctor."

"Please."

Kaida ran back. He put the boy on his back again and followed the crab. The crab had kept walking. In contrast to when he had seen it before, hunched down on the highway, it was walking quite briskly now. It made its way through the weeds and climbed over stones. The red-orange of its shell and claws sparkled in the sunlight. The air around it shimmered in the heat. It looked like a little mass of fierce determination.

The helicopter returned in a little less than an hour.

They brought a doctor. Kaida put the boy down. After examining the boy, the doctor gave him an injection.

"He should be brought to the hospital immediately."

The doctor was middle-aged. He looked deeply concerned.

"Is he going to die?" asked Kaida.

"I'm not saying he's going to die, but he's very sick."

"Then I'll carry him there."

The TV cameras were running.

"As a doctor, I have to tell you. You should give that up. You can follow the crab to the sea."

"But this kid is determined to do it himself."

"Are you prepared to take responsibility for him?"

Kaida was silent.

"Put him in the helicopter."

Kaida looked at the boy. The boy looked back at him with pleading eyes. He shook his head.

"All right. I'll take responsibility."

Kaida's heart leaped inside him.

"I'll take responsibility. If he dies, you can send me to prison or do whatever you want with me. I'm going to carry the boy to the sea. Just try taking him to the hospital. He may very well die there anyway. He buried his own grandfather and has come this far with the crab. This is the sixth day the crab's been walking. The sea is just ahead. Who can stop the crab? If you try, it'll bite you. It's the same with the kid. His parents abandoned him. His grandfather died. He doesn't have any friends. That dog and the crab are all he has. Why can't we let him follow the crab to the sea? It's the only thing he has to look forward to. It's all he has. Are you going to take that away from him too? All right, let's go, kid."

Kaida pulled the boy up onto his back.

"We're going to take some film of the crab." The cameraman followed the dog.

"Just a little. You hear?" Kaida shouted and wiped his forehead again.

Now he was in it to the end, thought Kaida. Whatever happened, happened.

After following the crab for a while, the cameraman left. The sound of the helicopter faded away.

"Thanks, mister."

"Forget about it. That doctor was a quack, anyway. Since when are you going to die from a little thing like a viper bite?"

"Yeah."

"Sleep for a while. I'm here, now. Let them bring it all on, I'm not afraid."

"You're tough, mister."

"I just talk tough." Kaida couldn't help but smile. The boy had shown what real toughness was.

The prefectural highway ran along the coastline. North of it was the Uchibō Line. Once you crossed that, the seashore was less than one kilometer away.

The crab arrived at the train tracks after three in the afternoon.

By that time Shin'ichi had climbed down from Kaida's back. He was walking, leaning on Kaida. His fever had gone down considerably. His thigh was just as swollen as before, but it wasn't as painful.

"So, what about the train tracks?" They were visible now. The crab was walking right up to them.

"As long as a train doesn't come…"

Shin'ichi didn't want to touch the crab if at all possible. The sea was so close. They'd gotten this far without him interfering.

"Okay, if a train comes, I'll stop it. Let's let her walk." Kaida didn't want to touch the crab, either. Kaida had walked with the crab for over six hours. In that time, he'd been surprised by the accuracy of the crab's instincts. Unless it came upon some particular obstacle, it was walking straight toward the sea. The sea was only one kilometer away. It would take several hours to walk that distance. It seemed to him that the crab was aware of this. It was down to the wire to arrive in time for high tide. Kaida thought he could detect an impatience in the crab's steps. Kaida had learned to interpret the crab's feelings.

The crab reached the train tracks. She effortlessly placed her legs on the rail. Her eye stalks were raised and it looked around. She slowly climbed over the rail. The dog followed. When the crab touched the second rail, she suddenly began to run. She was very quick. She climbed over the rail and ran into a clump of grass on the other side. She seemed like she was fleeing. As soon as Kaida and the boy crossed the tracks, they heard the sound of a train approaching.

Kaida realized that the crab had known that a train was coming.

"I don't think I can ever eat crab again," murmured Kaida. He imagined boiling and eating this crab. There was instinct inside the crab's shell. There was a very sharp awareness of danger. There was feeling, which could distinguish the boy and the dog from strangers. The idea of eating all of that made Kaida wince.

The crab walked about three hundred meters in an hour and a half. The prefectural highway came into sight at four-thirty.

A huge crowd had gathered along the highway.

"Rubberneckers…" mumbled Kaida when he saw them. At first he thought something must have happened. He quickly realized they had come to see the crab. A helicopter was hovering in the sky, filming the scene. They knew the course the crab was following. They'd been waiting.

A dozen or so men came running out of the crowd.

"What do you think you're doing?!" Kaida ran out, holding his arms out. They were newspaper photographers. He pushed one away.

"You're going to scare the crab. It's almost there now! Leave it alone, I tell you!"

"We most certainly will not," shouted the man he'd pushed. "Just take a look. There are almost a thousand people here. Several TV trucks are here to film the red-clawed crabs releasing their eggs. The police are here to control the crowds. The entire nation is watching this crab. Doesn't that mean something? All the people of Japan have been deeply moved by this crab's story. People will probably never look at animals in the same way again. We have a duty to report on that."

"What a load of crap!" shouted Kaida. "So everyone's going to be all emotional while they're tossing down slices of squid and octopus? They'll sit there with tears falling from their eyes while they're sucking on a crab claw? That's what people are like, and I could give a fuck about 'em. Don't make me laugh!"

Several police officers came running up.

"Stay away! Stay away, you idiots! Shit! Stop it! You're going to step on the crab!" Kaida went pale.

People were running down the highway.

"If that's what you think you're going to do, the boy will pick up the crab and take it to the sea. We won't let you see it!"

Kaida was terrified.

"Are you going to take the crab away from the boy and the dog? Is that the kind of cold-hearted bastards you are? Why do you think the boy and the dog have walked all this way with the crab? I'll kill anyone who tries to come near!"

Kaida picked up a stick.

"Now, wait just a minute." A man in late middle age stepped forward.

"I'm the mayor of this town. My name is Mita. We talked this over with the town police department and want to keep things peaceful and orderly. We're not equipped to turn all these people away, anyway. So how about this: we'll have everyone form two lines, and we can have the crab proceed between them."

"What are you saying, 'Have the crab proceed between them?'!" Kaida looked at him with a steely gaze.

"And so that's it? Just thank you and goodbye to the boy and the dog? This is as far as they can go? The town authorities and the crowds will take over from here? What the hell is this 'Have the crab proceed between them' shit?! And just so you know, a crab doesn't '*proceed*,' it crawls. And it goes where it wants. Try to remember that. That's enough. We don't need your help. We'll just have the boy pick up the crab. His grandfather told him to make sure the crab made it all the way to the sea on its own power, and that's what the boy's done up to here. He's never touched it. Now, when there are just a few steps to go, it's finished. And it's all your fault. This kid was bitten by a viper and almost died. But he still kept walking. Look at the dog! Even the dog is covered with blood from protecting the crab. Don't you have any decency? Why can't you just leave them alone? I see how it is. Goodbye to all of you. We won't show you the crab. If you want to see a crab, go catch one yourself and make it crawl for you. Use that for your show!"

Kaida walked up to the crab.

"Mister! Stop!" Shin'ichi screamed.

"Why? You didn't come all this way to put on a show for these jerks."

"I don't care either way. Let Aka walk to the sea. Mister, please. Don't pick her up."

Shin'ichi hopped over to Kaida on one foot and leaned on him.
"I promised Grandpa!"
"OK."
The boy's eyes were shining. Looking at them, Kaida nodded.
"That's right. You promised your grandpa. I think it was a terrible thing to make you promise, but…"
Kaida felt as if he could see the grandfather's eyes in Shin'ichi's. The face of an old man he's never seen before was there in the boy's eyes. He thought that's what he saw.

Shin'ichi walked, leaning on Kaida's shoulder.
Aka was heading toward the cliff along the sea shore. It was close to seven o'clock. It was already quite dark. Without the flashlight, Aka wasn't visible. In the beam of light, Aka's eye stalks were raised. They glittered like tiny jewels. She was heading toward the cliff with firmly anchored steps.
"Hey! Look at that!" Kaida hollered.
Shin'ichi saw it at the same time. In the flashlight's beam he saw a huge swarm of red-clawed crabs. It looked like thousands. They were moving in a swarm to the cliff that dropped straight to the sea. Aka approached the throng with her claws held high. She was a large scarlet crab. She entered the throng.
Kuro approached and wagged his tail. He was confused by the huge swarm of crabs. He stretched out his neck and sniffed, twitching his nose right and left as if searching for Aka's scent.
He soon gave up and came back next to Shin'ichi.
Kuro was angry. He was sad. He placed his paws on Shin'ichi's hips and whined.
"Let's go. Kuro."
Shin'ichi turned around. Shin'ichi was very sad, too. He felt as if Aka had betrayed him.
Kaida silently turned around.
The full moon emerged from behind the mountains.
Gentle waves were washing against the beach.
Shin'ichi, Kuro, and Kaida stood there on the shore. A crowd of people were nearby. The shore was filled with those who had come to watch. The steep cliff ran east and west. Flashlights flicked on

and off. All at once the television lights, connected by a cord to a generator some distance back from the beach, went on, bathing the cliff in light. It was as bright as day. A mass of red-clawed crabs was climbing down the cliff. Their claws and shells sparkled in the light. They glittered. The steep cliff was covered in countless glistening points of light moving down its surface.

It was a breathtaking sight. Silence reigned.

Shin'ichi didn't see red-clawed crabs. All he saw was light. You couldn't even say he saw that. The light was coming from inside his retinas.

Leading Kuro away, Shin'ichi left.

Shin'ichi and Kuro sat down on the shore.

"I know that Aka must have spawned, Kuro. She'll have lots of babies now, just like her."

The light of the full moon produced countless glimmering scales of light on the surface of the sea. They had moved away from where the red-clawed crabs were spawning. They couldn't hear the noise of the crowd. There was just the silent sea.

"Should we go home now, Kuro?"

He hugged Kuro's neck.

Somebody approached on the moonlit beach. It was impossible to tell if it was a man or a woman. It was a shimmering silver human form.

Sacred Creatures and the Demon-Hearted Woman

1

A red dirt road runs along the seacoast.

Sleet had just fallen, accumulating in the potholes, and as the wind blew across their surface, it created melancholy ripples.

A car was coming down the road.

A woman of about thirty was driving. Her face was pale, without a trace of color or life in it. She looked eaten away by illness.

The vast sea stretched out on her left. Leaden in color, several layers of clouds hung low over it. The water was so dark that it didn't reflect the clouds.

It was the Sea of Okhotsk in late October.

The woman didn't even look at the sea.

She had just passed Utoro, in the middle of the Shiretoko Peninsula. There wasn't much road beyond that point. You couldn't reach Shiretoko Cape by land.

The woman kept looking ahead. She seemed to be staring. She had a long face. Her lips were pressed together. She was gripping the steering wheel tightly. But her hands looked dead, too.

Her eyes, facing ahead, were dark.

Harsh winter scenery flashed by on both sides of the road. On one side was a cliff. The few tough weeds that grew there in summer were dead. The ground was brown. There was no green. From time to time a little gust of wind would shake the dead leaves and then disappear into the sea.

The sea was inert and heavy. The beach was covered with driftwood. The bones of trees. All of it bone white. The wind cut through it.

A little past Utoro, the road began to rise. Just before the rise, the woman slammed on the brakes.

She had seen something run across the road in front of her.

A feeling like anger floated across her face.

She got out of the car.

A cat was lying by the side of the road. The cat was trying desperately to escape from the giant steel monster that had hit it. It looked like its left front leg was broken. It was twisted into a strange shape. But that wouldn't be enough to deprive a cat of its nimbleness. It must have been hit somewhere else as well. It was floundering helplessly.

As it did so, it looked up at the woman.

Unexpected winter sunlight filled the cats two eyes. In them, the sun changed to yellow and sparkled.

"You little shithead," the woman said angrily. "It's your fault, you fucker."

She looked around. There was a stick nearby. She ran and picked it up. She was wearing jeans. She had long legs and a tight, high ass.

"Die, you little fucker."

She swung the stick. Her eyes were filled with hate. Her hair was wild and fell over her lifeless face. She hit the cat with all her might. She didn't know where the stick landed. She wasn't sure she felt the stick striking anything. The stick hit something soft and the hard earth at the same time. She lifted the stick up again. She held it with both hands. She brought it down again two or three times.

The woman tossed the stick aside.

Rivulets of thick perspiration rolled down her face. She looked at the cat. It was dead, covered in mud.

"It serves you right," she spat out.

She went back to her car and started it, sending it off with a violent jerk. Her hair was plastered to her forehead with perspiration, blocking her vision. She pushed her hair up with her right hand. Then she let out a short scream.

The car stopped suddenly.

She held her right hand out in front of her. Her hand enclosed a shank of her hair. The hair had come out in her hand when she pushed it up out of her eyes.

The woman's eyes were wide with terror. Her face was twisted in a horrid grimace. She sat there like that for some time. Gradually her eyes returned to normal. Then she closed them. The hair fell from her hand. It made a low rustling sound, like a tiny death rattle.

She rested her face against the steering wheel.

A blast of wind enveloped the car.

After a while the woman lifted her head. She hadn't been crying. Her eyes were like bottomless pools. They concealed something deep inside.

"The detective is following me," she murmured, looking at the windshield. The thought just suddenly came to her. She sensed that a detective from some police station was persistently on her trail. She saw his suspicious gaze. She even heard his footsteps approaching. The detective was in Utoro now. Eventually, he'd find the dead cat. He'd examine the body carefully.

"This is the work of Irako Nakase." She could hear the detective mutter those words.

She opened the car door.

She ran. Her long legs ran alongside the Okhotsk Sea.

She ran back to where the cat lay. She took off her coat and spread it out on the road. She tried to pick up the cat. The cat opened its eyes. It looked at her with its yellow eyes. The woman hesitated, and took a step back. The cat kept looking at her, as if entranced.

"All right." Her voice trembled.

She approached the cat again. She picked it up. She thought it might bite or scratch her, but it lay still. She wrapped it in her coat and ran back to the car.

A dilapidated hut stood on the beach.

It was once used by kelp harvesters. It was abandoned now and no one ever stayed there. The shack had wooden walls that had been patched here and there to keep out the drafts.

On the roof of the hut were truck tires that had washed up on the beach.

There were also a lot of stones on the roof.

Mount Iō was visible beyond the roof.

In front was a desolate and forlorn stretch of beach that led straight to the Sea of Okhotsk.

A single column of smoke rose from the hut.

The woman sat in front of the rusty stove. She was tending the cat. She had split a piece of driftwood to make a splint for its broken hind leg. She was quite handy at it. When she'd finished the splint, she examined the cat all over. There were no external wounds. The cat was opening and closing its eyes. It didn't seem to have the strength to even meow. It seemed to be mortally injured.

Cats have very tough skin, so they can be seriously hurt without showing external wounds. *It might well die*, the woman thought.

After she'd finished treating the cat, she went outside.

Night was approaching. The black sea seemed to foretell that. The horizon was not visible. It wasn't possible to tell if you were seeing clouds or water in the farthest distance. There were no boats on the water.

Several crows were sitting on stones on the beach. Their feathers were blowing in the wind.

The woman kept staring at the sea.

This was the second time she'd come to this hut. March last year. She'd come to see the ice floes at Shiretoko. She met a guy who was traveling at the time. He had the sunburned skin of a fisherman. He was walking, carrying a large backpack. He had a handsome face.

She met him at a diner in Utoro. The guy spoke to her first. She asked where he was going. The guy said he was going to a kelp harvester's hut way down the road. I'd like to see it, she said.

And so the guy showed her the way. The hut seemed about to be crushed by the ice floes. As far as you could see was one vast ice floe. It was a very strange sight, with the huge sheets of ice pushing up against and on top of each other. Some of them seemed to be biting the sky, like shark's teeth.

The guy fed some driftwood into the rusty stove.

The woman and the guy stood next to each other, looking at the ice floes.

He said he was staying in the hut overnight.

The woman didn't offer any indication of her intentions.

Before the sun set, the guy got on top of her. She didn't resist. She lay down and let him do what he wanted. He made love to her hungrily. What should I call you, she asked. Kaneo, he answered. Kaneo, I love you, she called out passionately as he made love to her. What's your name, he asked. Irako, the woman replied. You have a great body, Irako, he said.

He licked her sex until she was hoarse from crying out with pleasure.

They went their separate ways a little after noon the next day. They waved goodbye in Utoro.

The woman never asked the guy's last name. She wanted to, but she was afraid it would only bring him misfortune. She had sex with him three times. When they parted ways, she could still feel his hard cock in her cunt. Enjoying that feeling, she left Utoro, which was teeming with tourists.

She never thought she'd come to that hut again.

There was no one here this time.

No one would come here at this time of year. The ice floes arrived in late January. They melted and disappeared by April. Tourists still came to Shiretoko in the summer. But only until late September. By November, Shiretoko lost all its interest. No one went there.

The abandoned hut stood there lost in a state of timeless eternity.

The woman looked at the sea.

It was a melancholy scene, one that would dissolve your soul.

2

The man was dead.

There's a lighthouse at Sunosaki Cape at the extreme southern tip of the Bōsō Peninsula. The man's body was on the beach, at the foot of a cliff not far from the lighthouse.

It was discovered at 10:00 a.m. on October 30.

The Tateyama Police Department examined the body and decided it was a suicide.

The man left a note.

It was filled with hatred.

Irako Nakase is a demon.
She has a demon in her heart.
That demon killed my entire family.
I had to take revenge.
The demon will die a hideous death in a month. It will die without fail. I made sure of it.

The note was hastily written.

The man included his name and address.

It was Tomonari Shimada, resident of Setagaya Ward, Tokyo.

The Tateyama Police contacted the Tokyo Metropolitan Police.

The Setagaya Police Department found out that Tomonari Shimada was a physician. He'd worked at the Setagaya Chōsei Clinic.

When they found out it was Tomonari Shimada, the entire Setagaya Criminal Investigation Department was stunned.

On June 20, three months earlier, Tomonari Shimada's wife, Hiroko, and their son, Tomoyuki, had committed suicide. They had jumped in front of an Odakyū Line train. The driver of the train confirmed that it was suicide. Hiroko ran onto the tracks carrying her infant son Tomoyuki.

The reason for the suicide was clear right away.

Dr. Shimada had been accused of malpractice.

A six-year-old boy, Yutaka Maeno, who was under his care, had died at the end of April. Yutaka had been hospitalized for asthma. His symptoms were quite severe. His parents were grief stricken, but they had to accept their son's death.

But then a complication arose.

One day in mid-May, the dead boy's mother, Yoshie, stormed into the hospital in a frenzy. Though a nurse tried to restrain her, she broke free and charged into the office of Dr. Kemi, the hospital director. The director had someone else in the office at the time. Yoshie grabbed the hospital director and shouted, "Give me back Yutaka! I want my son back alive!"

With the help of the guest, Director Kemi was able to subdue Yoshie.

When he heard what she had to say, the director was dumbfounded.

Last night someone had made an anonymous phone call to Yoshie's home. It was a woman's voice. Your child didn't die, he was killed, said the woman.

That night, Dr. Shimada was the doctor on duty in the pediatrics ward. He was also Yutaka Maeno's supervising physician. But when Yutaka had an asthma attack, Shimada wasn't at the hospital. A nurse searched for him in a panic. He'd said he was going for a drink at a local bar. But when she called the bar, it turned out he hadn't been there that night.

By the time one of the internal medicine physicians rushed to the scene, it was too late to save the child.

He died.

Shimada returned to the hospital an hour after the boy's death. He'd been drinking. And not only that. He'd been at a nearby love hotel from seven to nine o'clock. He was with a nurse from the same hospital. She was off duty that day, and she had met up with Shimada at the love hotel.

Shimada was thirty-seven years old. He was handsome and popular with women.

If Shimada had been at the hospital, the boy could have been saved. Shimada had violated the code of medical ethics. It was completely unforgiveable for a physician to leave the hospital while on duty to have sex with a nurse. The boy had died because he'd been out drinking and screwing a nurse.

The accusations went on.

Shimada was also an obstetrician. Shimada often violated patient confidentiality. When he operated on elderly women he would say the only way he could stand to do it was to be drunk. And in fact he often did perform surgery under the influence of alcohol.

The anonymous tipster said all of this.

When Yoshie Maeno had finished speaking, the hospital director was pale. He didn't know a thing about any of this. He promised to get to the bottom of the matter and sent Yoshie Maeno home.

Two days later, Director Kemi asked the Maenos to come to the hospital to see him.

He had investigated the matter fully, he said, and nothing was amiss. The anonymous caller was just someone who had a grudge against Dr. Shimada and was slandering him to ruin his career. Dr. Shimada had been in the hospital's break room the entire time. When he was called, he went immediately to treat the boy. He did everything in his power. That was the truth, stated Kemi.

Several days later Yoshie Maeno showed up at Dr. Shimada's house dressed in mourning.

When Shimada's wife Hiroko answered the door, Yoshie screamed, "Give me back my child!" Hiroko panicked and closed the door. Hiroko had heard the general outlines of the incident from her husband. Hiroko believed Shimada. This whole thing about running off to a love hotel with a nurse while on duty was just too far fetched.

Yoshie was outside the door screaming. She had a Buddhist rosary in her hands. Shaking the beads, she kept wailing and calling: "Your husband slipped out of the hospital on his night shift to go to a hotel and fuck one of his nurses! Because of that, my son died! He was killed! Give me back my child! Give me back Yutaka! Give me back my Yutaka!"

Yoshie's eyes were fierce and wild. Her pale face was frightening. She seemed to have lost her mind. She continued screaming the same thing over and over in a shrill voice.

A crowd gathered. Yoshie paid no attention to them. She stamped her feet with vexation, clasped her rosary, and kept on screaming.

She was a small woman. Her entire being seemed to be a concentrated mass of maternal despair for a lost child. She was filled with an unquenchable grief that no amount of shouting could exhaust.

Pressing her hands over her ears, Hiroko called the police.

A patrol car came, picked up Yoshie, and left.

Three days later Yoshie returned, wearing the same mourning dress. It had been raining lightly since the morning. Yoshie stood in front of the house without an umbrella. Her clothes dripping, she screamed the same things as before.

In tears, Hiroko called the police again.

Detective Tokuda of the Criminal Investigation Department was in the police car this time.

Tokuda was in his fifties. While taking Yoshie back home, he listened to her story. He knew the basic outlines from the previous occasion they'd sent a squad car to get her. It was not a situation for police involvement. If there was clear evidence of criminal malpractice, things would have been different, but determining whether medical treatment was timely or not was a difficult call to make.

But now that things had escalated to this point, their hand was forced. Whether or not there was any substance to Yoshie Maeno's accusations, her son's death had driven her to this extreme. If they let things go on like this, there was a distinct possibility it might lead to an unpleasant, even violent, incident.

Tokuda dropped Yoshie off at her home and headed toward the hospital.

He met with the hospital director, Dr. Kemi, as well as with Dr. Shimada and the nurses on duty that night, questioning them each about the sequence of events.

He went back to the hospital for the next two days.

Tokuda was known for the persistence of his investigations.

After several days, Tokuda had gathered most of the facts. It was still not a case that called for police involvement. When the boy Yutaka Maeno's condition worsened, Dr. Shimada was *not* at the hospital. This was not the testimony of anyone at the hospital. The doctors and nurses all reported precisely what the hospital director had told them to. It was clear to Tokuda that they had all been coached.

The problem, however, was with the internist who had treated the boy when he had his seizure. He was a middle-aged doctor named Yanagizawa. At the time, Yanagizawa was in the doctors' office, playing *go* with a pharmaceutical company representative. He dashed immediately to the pediatrics ward. Yanagizawa told Tokuda that he had done everything he could. There's not much difference between the expertise of an internist and a pediatrician. The only difference was that he was not the boy's supervising physician.

Yanagisawa read the boy's chart and treated him accordingly. Yanagizawa stated that it was true that Shimada was not present at the time. But he got there twenty minutes after Yanagizawa did. It hadn't been a problem.

Not only the drug company rep, but also the nurses and patients he encountered all testified that Yanagizawa went to the pediatrics ward. And Yanagizawa had a good reputation at the hospital.

It was, after all, not a matter for police involvement.

Dealing with Shimada's lapse in professional ethics as a physician was up to the hospital. The claims of the Maeno family should properly be addressed by negotiations between the family and the hospital.

Tokuda focused on finding out who made the anonymous call. If the woman could be identified, the truth would be easily discovered.

Six nurses were on duty that night. The pediatrics ward is on the fourth floor. The internal medicine wing is on the same floor. It seemed to him that one of those six nurses must have made the call. Or one of them talked about what happened to another person, and that person made the call.

But he couldn't find out who it was.

Dr. Shimada was also stumped. He said he couldn't think of any reason why any of the nurses should have something against him.

Tokuda met with Yoshie Maeno.

He reported on the results of the investigation and tried to persuade her to stop harassing the Shimada family. If she was determined not to forgive Dr. Shimada, she should consult an attorney, he said.

Yoshie Maeno agreed.

That was the end of the matter, thought Tokuda.

But before a month had passed, Dr. Shimada's wife had taken their young son and killed herself by jumping in front of a train.

Tokuda met with Shimada.

Shimada was in a daze, staring emptily into space. No matter what Tokuda asked, he made no effort to respond. Tokuda sat there silently for more than an hour, waiting for Shimada to speak voluntarily.

After a long time, Shimada started to talk.

Hiroko had had a breakdown, he said softly. She said that the people in the neighborhood were all looking at her suspiciously.

Their gazes were accusing, saying that they knew her husband had slipped out while on duty to have sex with a nurse, and he let a patient die as a result. When she took Tomoyuki anywhere, she heard people whispering that the Shimadas had let another child die but look how well they care for their own son.

It was a neurosis, said Shimada. In fact, people hadn't treated him any differently. He prescribed medication for his wife. But she became more and more depressed. She refused to go out shopping. She locked herself in the house, and when Shimada got home she hadn't cooked any dinner, she would just be sitting there with the lights off.

Shimada thought of moving. If he could transfer somewhere else for a month or two, the illness that had consumed Yoshie Maeno's mind might burn itself out.

Right after he suggested that to his wife, she committed suicide.

"That witch Maeno. That murderer," murmured Shimada into empty space.

Tokuda listened to his words with a feeling of doom.

And then Dr. Shimada committed suicide by throwing himself off a cliff.

"Irako Nakase?" whispered Tokuda to himself.

3

Irako Nakase worked as a nurse at the Setagaya Chōsei Clinic.

Detective Tokuda went to see Irako Nakase at the clinic on October 4, the day after the news had come in from the Tateyama Police Department.

Irako Nakase had taken the day off without permission. She'd been away from work for the last six days. He found that out when he spoke to the head nurse. Irako Nakase lived in an apartment in Higashi Kitazawa. The head nurse had called three times, but Irako hadn't picked up.

Tokuda made an appointment with the hospital director Kemi.

Tomonari Shimada's suicide had been reported in the papers, but the articles had not included his statement of intent to wreak vengeance on Irako Nakase.

He had written that he would avenge himself, that Irako would die within a month.

The note seemed to imply that she was still alive. He had to investigate the matter with the utmost haste.

Tokuda explained the contents of the note to Kemi.

Kemi listened, his hands folded on the table in front of him. His fingers were shaking ever so slightly.

When Tokuda had finished his explanation, he looked at Kemi. The director's hair was about half white. He had a dignified face that suggested a good upbringing. He seemed pained.

"Is there anything you can tell me? Is there, for example, some drug that would kill someone in a month's time?"

Dr. Shimada hadn't been to the hospital since his wife's suicide on June 20. He was still officially employed there; he was on a temporary leave of absence.

Irako had disappeared seven days ago. In other words, she had been working as usual up through September 27. Shimada's revenge on Irako must have taken place at about the time that Irako stopped coming to work. Shimada took his revenge, then killed himself, and now Irako, who knew that she could not escape her fate, had disappeared.

They were a doctor and a nurse, so if he had used some drug, it would have to be something for which there was no treatment.

Tokuda thought that the Setagaya Chōsei Clinic must have been the scene of this act of revenge.

When Shimada's wife and child committed suicide, Shimada's anger was directed at Yoshie Maeno. He cursed her, called her a witch and a murderer. Tokuda had worried at the time that Shimada might try to retaliate against Yoshie.

But instead, he identified the woman who had made the anonymous phone call. How he had identified her, Tokuda didn't know, but he had pinned it down to Irako Nakase, a nurse who worked at the same hospital.

Tokuda felt a sense of nagging regret. Earlier when he had been investigating who had made the call, one of the nurses on duty that night had been Irako Nakase. If he had learned that she was the caller, he would have been able to prevent this entire thing from happening.

But it wasn't as if the entire incident hinged on identifying the anonymous caller by whatever means required. He'd let that drop, Tokuda had said to himself, and had stopped his investigation.

There was no physical relationship between Shimada and Irako. If there had been, Shimada would have suspected Irako from the start. But Shimada had said he had no idea who had made the call. Irako was twenty-eight. She wasn't a beauty, but Tokuda remembered that she had a certain appeal. When he'd talked with her, his impression was that she was cold, but she didn't seem like a woman who would snitch on others, he remembered thinking.

The words of the head nurse backed up that impression.

When she learned that it was Irako who had made the call and that Shimada had taken some kind of revenge on her, she seemed startled. Irako had only worked at the clinic for about half a year. She never smiled, but she wasn't devious. The head nurse looked like she didn't believe Tokuda. No wonder Shimada hadn't had any suspicion, thought Tokuda.

It had taken Shimada more than three months to identify the anonymous caller. That was an indication of just how little an impression Irako had made on him.

Why did she do it?

Was it some sense of justice, outrage at a doctor's lack of professional ethics?

Or did she have a relationship with Shimada after all?

Tokuda was interested in this.

She's a demon, Shimada had written. *She was a woman with a demon in her heart.*

Those words made him assume that Irako was no ordinary woman.

"I can't think of any drug that would have that effect," said Kemi solemnly.

Tokuda knew what was going through Kemi's mind. The reputation of Setagaya Chōsei Clinic was going to suffer serious harm because of recent events. The death of Yutaka Maeno would be reinvestigated. This time Tokuda would have to conduct the most rigorous investigation. When he did, it would come out that Dr. Shimada had indeed been having sex with a nurse from the hospital at a love hotel while the boy was undergoing his fatal seizure.

The moral and ethical responsibility of Kemi, who had swept that fact under the rug, would also be called into question.

"If it's not a drug, what do you think Dr. Shimada used?"
Tokuda took out a cigarette.
"I...can't really say."
He shook his head, then seemed to have an idea, and he looked at Tokuda.
"What?"
"Maybe cobalt," he said with what sounded like a moan.
"Cobalt?"
"Yes."
Kemi wiped his forehead with the back of his hand.

The Setagaya Chōsei Clinic had a radiotherapy room. It was used in treating cancer. If Shimada had brought Irako into the radiotherapy room, then the "within one month" in his suicide note would make sense.

"But could someone do that? Irako was a nurse. She wouldn't allow herself to be exposed to radiation."

"Yes, that's the problem."

If she had cried out, people would hear. If he had irradiated her, it would have to have been a night when she was on duty, and people would have heard her scream.

Of course he could have tied her up and gagged her, but it would be dangerous to attempt that in the hospital.

But it wasn't impossible, either. If Shimada had been willing to expose himself to the radiation at the same time, there would have been no problem. The key for the radiotherapy room was kept in the office. It would have been easy for Shimada to take it. Somehow or other he turned off the warning switch. He entered the room. Then he could open the shutter to the radiation machine, tell Irako he had something private to tell her, and get her into the room.

With the shutter open, the cobalt rays were being released into the room. They didn't make any noise or produce any light, so they wouldn't be noticed. Soon the entire room would be contaminated with gamma rays.

People rarely came near the radiotherapy room, so it was the ideal place for a clandestine meeting. The nurse would feel safe going there.

Shimada brings Irako into the room and stays there talking to her for ten or fifteen minutes. If he had been asking her about the anonymous phone call, she would probably have left the room, so he must have pretended that he had fallen for her and tried to talk her into having sex with him. Irako agreed. All that time, the entire room was being bombarded with radioactive cobalt rays. They were completely exposed.

After he judged enough time had passed, Shimada sends Irako back out. When the contamination level exceeds 400 roentgens, one experiences headache and dizziness. Cobalt radiation can be used with relative safety when directed only at the cancer, but if the entire body is exposed to 400 roentgens, death follows in just two or three hours. That wouldn't be revenge. At half that dose, 200 roentgens, Irako wouldn't notice anything right away. That's what Shimada must have done.

After Irako leaves the room, Shimada closes the shutter. The contamination quickly disappears.

Shimada leaves the hospital.

About an hour after being fully exposed to radiation, one experiences headache, dizziness, and nausea. It's like morning sickness. It's called radiation intoxication. That's when Irako would have noticed she'd been exposed. Shimada could have waited until about this time and called Irako. You have only one month left to live, he'd say.

There would be nothing Irako could do. There was no cure.

In about a week her hair would begin to fall out in clumps. She'd lose her appetite, and purple blotches would appear all over her body. She'd have a fever. She'd feel heavy and lethargic.

In two weeks she'd develop ulcers all over her body. She would ache everywhere and experience piercing, bone-wrenching pains.

By the third week, the mucous membrane inside her mouth begins to disintegrate. The saliva and phlegm become mixed with blood. The eyesight begins to dim.

The fourth week is even worse. She would become extremely anemic and lose all color, down to her fingernails. She'd be too weak to stand, she'd start hemorrhaging from her genitals, and her urine would be mixed with blood. She couldn't stand up.

Of course, she'd grow thin as a ghost. The pall of death would quickly envelop her body.

There are minor individual differences, but generally in a little over a month she would be plucked by the angel of death.

Death is unavoidable.

There could be no crueler vengeance. But given that Shimada had written that Irako had only a month to live, it seemed almost one hundred percent certain that he had exposed her to radioactive cobalt. It was unthinkable that a drug could achieve that result.

Kemi's legs were trembling slightly. Now the police would conduct a full-scale investigation. If anyone had seen Shimada at the hospital on the last night Irako was on duty, it was all over. Or if anyone had witnessed symptoms of radiation intoxication in Irako. It would no longer be possible to stonewall.

In the worst-case scenario, the hospital would have to shut down for a time.

Kemi looked down at the table.

Tokuda left the hospital and made his way to Higashi Kitazawa.

He continued to envision Kemi's description of what might have gone on in the radiotherapy room.

His conjecture was right on the nose. Checking with a nurse, he discovered that Irako had experienced radiation intoxication. It happened the night before she stopped coming to work. After 9:00 p.m. that night, she had vomited. She said she felt dizzy. The doctor on duty examined her and suggested she might be pregnant. After a short time, she went off work and left the hospital.

He also found that Shimada had come to the hospital that night. He had been doing that occasionally, even though he wasn't working.

The following day, Irako stopped going to work.

The picture in Tokuda's mind was of Shimada and Irako in each other's embrace in the radiotherapy room, being bombarded by radioactive cobalt. He could see her white legs wrapped around the man. The gamma rays penetrating her healthy skin, minute after minute. Her full head of hair shaking as he fucked her. The hair that would silently fall out just a week later.

He envisioned a scene of raw, unbridled, savage lust—a demonic embrace.

What was Shimada thinking as he penetrated her?

It was a terrible revenge, at the cost of his own life.

4

Irako Nakase lived in the Summer Breeze Apartments, a small, two-story building. Irako's apartment was on the first floor. It consisted of a six-mat room, a three-mat room, a kitchen, a toilet, and a bath. The rent was fifty-five thousand yen a month.

Of course she wasn't home.

Tokuda talked to the middle-aged woman who was the superintendent.

Her name was Eiko Koizumi. She didn't have any idea where Irako had gone either. She seemed to have left several days ago, she said.

"So, she's done something wrong, then," said Koizumi with a scowl.

"What do you mean by that," asked Tokuda.

"Well, now that you ask," began Koizumi, as if she had expected it.

Tokuda didn't look like your typical detective. He had a friendly face. He rarely showed anger. He spoke in a pleasant manner. It made people want to talk to him.

"She's a very nasty piece of work," said Koizumi quietly. "Now that you mention it, about a month ago another man was here asking about her."

"A month ago?"

"Yes. He asked what kind of a person she was."

"And?"

"I told him that she was a very scary woman." She looked around.

Irako Nakase moved into the apartment at the end of the previous year. She was single. She said she was a nurse. It would be reassuring to have a nurse living in the apartment house, Koizumi thought, and she tried to ingratiate herself with the new tenant. But she soon stopped speaking to Irako. One day, less than ten days after Irako had moved in, she came to Koizumi with a complaint.

Mr. and Mrs. Kuwano, who lived directly above her, had a cat. Irako wanted Koizumi to make them get rid of it.

Cats attract fleas, lice, and other pests. And the cat came onto Irako's veranda. It shed and it was dirty, she said.

Koizumi was stumped. The Kuwanos were elderly. They'd had the cat for four years. They had found it as a little kitten on the street. It was on the verge of death, and they'd taken it in and cared for it. Koizumi was startled by the steely coldness with which Irako demanded she tell the couple to get rid of their cat.

When Koizumi hesitated, Irako pressed her, asking, Doesn't the rental contract mean anything? Koizumi had no reply to that. The rental contract did prohibit keeping any animals, even birds.

Koizumi said she'd talk to the Kuwanos. Of course they wouldn't get rid of that cat. They loved it like a child.

Irako's cold-heartedness frightened Koizumi. Here she was making a complaint less than ten days after she'd moved in. No, not a complaint—a demand. She seemed to have no awareness that Koizumi had tried to treat her with special consideration up to then. *This woman is scary*, thought Koizumi.

Koizumi said that she never saw Irako smile. Smiles are the lubricant that makes human relationships run smoothly. Her refusal to smile seemed to indicate her rejection of any form of interaction. Her face was neither beautiful nor ugly. But she had a lovely body—enough to make Koizumi envious. Her legs, especially, were long. And she had a well-shaped behind.

Koizumi thought it strange she had no boyfriends. But she also felt she understood why.

Koizumi talked to the Kuwanos.

The Kuwanos were very upset.

Then one night, about fifteen days later, a terrible thing happened. It was raining that night. In the middle of the night, Koizumi heard a cat screech horribly. She got up and opened the window. It seemed that the screeching was coming from the courtyard. But she couldn't see anything.

The Kuwanos came to her office. They had heard the cat scream. They went out with Koizumi to search the yard with a flashlight.

There was no cat to be seen.

The Kuwanos' cat was named Kuro. Kuro didn't come home the next night or the next. The Kuwanos were afraid. They suggested that Irako had killed their cat. The elderly couple didn't have the nerve to go pounding on Irako's door and demand to know what she'd done with their cat. Nor could they really go to the police for help. They were just afraid and helpless.

Thinking that Kuro had been killed, they couldn't eat for days.

But then Kuro came home.

Six days had passed since he'd disappeared. When they saw him, they gasped in horror. From his back to his left side there was a huge scar. The skin was peeling off and hanging in twists from the wound. There was no fur. The festering skin was hideous.

He was incredibly thin.

The couple called a veterinarian. The vet took one look at the cat and said that someone had thrown boiling water on it. The skin would never heal. The fur would never grow back. Surgery would do no good.

The Kuwanos trembled at such an act of cruelty.

They knew it was Irako's doing. But they hadn't witnessed it. Irako had waited for the cat to walk along her veranda and then thrown boiling water at it.

Irako was a nurse. She knew what happened to an animal when you threw boiling water on it. She was fully aware it would turn into a keloid scar that would never heal. The thought that she knew that, that she boiled the water in advance, and then sat there waiting for the cat to pass by on her veranda, was horrifying.

She was a demon.

After several days, Kuro disappeared again. This time he didn't come back. The veterinarian said that he probably died. The scar was too large. All living things, including human beings, die when one third of their skin is burned. The cat must have known what was in store for it and gone off to die.

The Kuwanos wrote a posthumous Buddhist name for the cat on a strip of wood and placed it on their family altar. The only thing they could do was join their hands in prayer and hope their cat was now at peace.

Irako acted as if nothing had happened.

She started working at the hospital from about the end of February. She wasn't friendly with anyone living in the apartment building.

About a month after she started working at Setagaya Chōsei Clinic, another frightening event took place.

A family living in a house on the way from the apartment building to the train station had a shiba inu dog. It barked a lot. The gate to the house was made of iron. The dog always sat there and barked at passersby whom it didn't like.

One day when Koizumi was out shopping she noticed three policemen at the house. There was something going on. She approached and asked what had happened. The homeowner, her face red and swollen from crying, explained that someone had thrown poisoned meatballs into the yard and killed Poochy.

Koizumu felt a chill run down her spine.

She had seen the dog barking at Irako once. It had bared its fangs in hatred. The dog barked at many people, but it never bared its fangs. A dog bares it fangs when it's cornered or facing someone who has mistreated it.

Irako couldn't have mistreated the dog through the iron fence. More likely, thought Koizumi, the dog could smell the demon that lived in Irako's heart. This was a woman who would wait in the middle of the night with a pot of boiling water to throw on a cat. The dog must have been able to sense instinctively the demon residing within Irako.

Irako was the one who tossed in the poison meatballs. No other person would be cruel enough.

Koizumi realized that she had rented an apartment to a demon.

She conferred with her husband. Wasn't there some way to get her to leave? But of course there was no easy way of managing that. She just had to bear it.

Koizumi explained all of this to Tokuda.

Tokuda walked to the station.

He had gotten a key from the superintendent and entered Irako's apartment. He'd looked for something that might tip him off as to where she'd gone. But he found nothing. There wasn't a single letter. No bank book. The room had been neatly tidied.

There was nothing in it suggesting death.

But he wasn't completely without leads. Irako had gotten a divorce about a year and a half ago. Tokuda found that out at the ward office. After the divorce, she moved into the Summer Breeze Apartments.

Surely there was a possibility that her former husband knew something useful.

Tokuda was beginning to form his own picture of Irako.

Irako had made the anonymous phone call accusing Shimada. She and Shimada had no relationship at that point. If they had, Shimada would have immediately suspected her as the anonymous caller. But it took Shimada three months to identify her. As demonstrated by the surprise of the head nurse, no one had suspected Irako.

But Irako had done it. Tokuda thought that she had probably told Yoshie Maeno the truth. She may have exaggerated a little. But the actual facts were no doubt quite close to her account.

Irako hadn't reported on Shimada out of anger at his unprofessional or unethical behavior. She simply enjoyed watching people suffer. She wanted to watch Shimada wriggle in pain. That was her only motive. That's why it took so long to find out it was her.

Irako Nakase is a demon.
She has a demon in her heart.

Those words from Shimada's note said it all, he thought. Shimada had worked desperately to find out who had made the call. When he found out it was Irako, Shimada was puzzled. He couldn't understand what would motivate her to do it. He found out more about her. The man who asked about her at the Summer Breeze Apartments about a month ago must have been Shimada. As he checked her out, he discovered what a frightening woman she was. She hadn't reported on him out of any righteous outrage, but just because she wanted to entrap another person. The result was that she drove his wife and child to suicide.

She's a demon, moaned Shimada. This woman has a demon inside her, he called out in his mind. She was a demon who delighted in the suffering of others.

Shimada decided to take his revenge. He decided that he'd also die by exposing himself to radioactive cobalt, but he'd take his vengeance against Irako in the process. Shimada opened the shutter of the cobalt machine to burn the demon to death. That demon deep inside her could only be killed by full exposure to gamma rays.

A demon, whispered Tokuda to himself.

It seemed a very symbolic method of revenge.

And now where had the demon who'd been blasted with gamma rays holed up?

5

Ikuo Kimura, who had been married to Irako Nakase, lived in Nogata, Nakano Ward. He had a job at an accounting firm. He was a small man. He was thirty-two, four years older than Irako. Kimura flushed when Tokuda said he wanted to ask about Irako.

"Whatever she's done, it has nothing to do with me," he replied to Tokuda. He looked frightened.

"Do you think she's done something?" Tokuda hadn't explained why he was there.

Kimura was silent.

Then Tokuda explained. He told him that Irako had been exposed to fatal cobalt radiation and had probably gone off somewhere to die. It would be a short trip. He asked if Kimura had any idea where she might go.

Kimura shook his head. He didn't look up.

"Can you tell me something?" asked Tokuda. He told him what he'd heard from Koizumi, about the cat at the Summer Breeze Apartments and the neighborhood dog. He told him about the events at Setagaya Chōsei Clinic, including the anonymous phone call and the tragic deaths it had triggered. There was no proof that Irako was the culprit in any of them. The only clear indication was that Dr. Shimada had accused Irako and then killed himself. Even the exposure to the radioactive cobalt was a conjecture.

Kimura's testimony would decide whether Irako Nakase was the suspect. Or it would make her involvement unlikely.

It was important testimony.

"Do you think I have the wrong idea about Irako Nakase? Shimada said that a demon lived inside her. I suspect he was telling the truth." Tokuda looked at Kimura, whose gaze remained on the floor.

"Yes." After a short pause, he nodded. It was a grim nod. "I don't think you have the wrong idea about her. Probably not." Kimura lowered his gaze to the table. But he wasn't looking at the table. A vast blackness had opened up before his eyes.

Kimura had said, "Probably not." But he didn't mean it. There was no probability about it. Tokuda's description was spot on.

Two years earlier Irako had killed another cat by dousing it with boiling water. At the time, the Kimuras were living in a little rented house in Nerima Ward.

A pet cat from somewhere in the neighborhood often crossed their yard. It was a small yard, but sparrows and starlings often came there. The cat would hunt them. It would hide in the shade, repositioning its feet again and again, flicking its tail slightly. The next instant it would leap out like a black bullet. Even so, it rarely caught anything. Kimura enjoyed watching it.

Sometimes he threw the cat scraps of food.

One day Irako saw the cat hunting a sparrow. As she watched, her expression changed. She threw a nearby plastic tray at the cat. The tray missed the cat and hit a tree, slicing off a branch.

"What are you doing?" asked Kimura angrily.

He knew she hated animals. She hated dogs and cats and birds. Kimura didn't know why. Irako didn't talk much. Nor did she seem to have any desire to justify herself to anyone. She never made any excuses for her actions. When she decided not to talk, she wouldn't say a word. She looked at Kimura coldly.

They had gotten married the year before. The first year, Kimura didn't realize what her personality was like. She had a really beautiful body. Kimura was in its thrall. He only paid attention to her physical appearance.

Irako liked sex, too. They spent their days in sweaty embraces. Kimura would do whatever she asked. If she said she hated animals, that was okay with him. In spite of that—or maybe it was all part of the same thing—she loved to eat meat that was almost raw. Kimura liked his meat well done. Irako told him to eat it the same way she did. He did as he was told. Kimura was weak. He couldn't argue with people. He never stood up to Irako. She became the dominant figure in the relationship.

But her throwing the tray at the cat made him angry.

Irako didn't answer. She ignored him. For the first time, he grabbed her. "Hey," he said, and grabbed her shoulder. She spun around and slapped him. Her palm made a loud smacking sound as it hit his cheek. Kimura felt dizzy and fell back against the wall. Irako kicked out at him, hitting him on the shin, and he fell backward on his ass.

He didn't really remember what happened after that. In the end he was pinned down on the floor and was soundly beaten. He tried to fight back, but he was no match for her. Irako was taller than he was and stronger than she looked. They grappled, she flipped him to the ground over her hip, and things took a very frightening turn as the violence escalated. If he had stooped to biting and clawing he might have been able to hold his own, but he couldn't bring himself to do that.

She climbed on his back and beat him until his face was red and swollen.

Kimura surrendered.

Irako killed the cat four days later. She wasn't working that day. Kimura came home after work that evening. As he stood in front of the entryway to the house, he heard a cat screech horribly. He ran inside. Irako was standing on the veranda facing the yard. She had a bucket with steam rising from it. The cat was writhing at her feet. Steam was rising from the cat.

Kimura stopped in his tracks.

He realized at a glance that she had thrown the boiling water on the cat. Irako was staring at it. Her face in profile was expressionless, like a Noh mask. Her pale visage face was focused on the cat's agony.

Kimura was speechless.

The cat screeched only once. After that it simply rolled to the right and the left, like a ball on fire. Gradually the motion subsided, and finally it was still.

Silently Irako went back to the kitchen. She got a large plastic bag and deftly nudged the cat into it with her foot.

Kimura watched, trembling.

I've got to leave her, he decided. He'd miss her body, but he was terrified of her heart. She wasn't human. She was a demon. Someday she'd end up killing him, he thought.

That night Irako sought Kimura out for sex. In the four days up to then, she hadn't let him touch her. Kimura had no desire to. But if he were to refuse, she would have hit him. He had to do as she asked. She sat on top of him and had her way with him.

When it was over, Kimura asked why she'd done such a horrific thing. Cats are filthy and carry germs, she replied.

That didn't convince Kimura. He told her then and there that he wanted a divorce.

Fine with me, replied Irako. There was no emotion in her voice. She felt contempt for Kimura, who was a plain-looking man. Kimura knew she hadn't married him because she liked him. It had been an arranged marriage. It was Kimura who had fallen for her. Kimura knew that he had fallen for a woman with a monstrous nature.

But they didn't get divorced right away.

They stayed together for another six months.

One night there was a traffic accident near their house. An old woman was hit by a car. She wasn't that badly hurt. Rather than hit, she'd just been knocked down.

The car didn't stop. The old woman didn't see what kind of car it was. She didn't remember the license plate number. The police investigated at the scene of the accident, but they didn't find any traces of paint or other evidence that would help identify the driver.

The police went through the neighborhood asking if anyone had seen anything.

They came to the Kimuras' house, too. The accident had taken place before 8:00 p.m. Kimura and Irako had been watching television, so naturally they said they didn't know anything.

Kimura had a few drinks and went to bed after ten. It was just a few drinks, to help him get to sleep. That night, too, he fell asleep after about thirty minutes.

A sound woke him up.

In the living room, Irako was talking to someone. She was speaking in a low voice. Irako had gone to bed at the same time as Kimura. Kimura listened, wondering who on earth she was talking to in the middle of the night.

Irako was making an anonymous call to the police. She said the name of the driver and hung up the phone.

Kimura pretended to be sleeping.

He knew he had to divorce her now. Irako had named a local housewife. She was a beautiful young woman in her mid-twenties. She'd just gotten married, it seemed. Kimura often saw her walking side by side with her husband through the neighborhood.

Of course she hadn't done it. Irako had been watching television when the accident took place.

Kimura felt a chill run through his body.

Irako didn't even know the woman. Irako refused to get involved with any of the neighbors. At most, she may have passed the woman on the street. And yet, she called the police and blamed the accident on her.

She was jealous of the woman's looks. There could be no other reason. The woman had a light complexion and was tall. She stood out. She turned men's heads. Her face was almost too perfect.

And she drove a red sports car.

Irako tiptoed back into bed.

Soon he heard her breathing softly in her sleep.

What a horrifying woman, thought Kimura.

He couldn't stop shaking for some time.

The next morning, when he was on his way to work, Kimura saw a police car in front of the woman's house.

That night he learned that the police had taken her to the station. Irako told him. They brought her in for questioning and then took her back home before noon. The forensics team examined her car. She didn't have an alibi. She said she was watching television with her husband, but his corroboration didn't carry much weight. They found no evidence that her car had been involved in an accident, but how would they when she'd only knocked over the old woman. There wasn't anything else the police could do, apparently, said Irako.

Then she added: "But I know she did it."

Uh-huh, replied Kimura.

They got divorced about a month later.

6

The first snow fell in Shiretoko in early November.

About five centimeters fell, but it melted in a few days. It began snowing on and off from mid-month. Yōkichi Kitami went to take a look at the kelp harvester's hut on a day when it had been snowing since the morning. Yōkichi didn't care about the hut. Yōkichi was looking for a bear. The area along the seashore near the hut was this particular bear's territory.

It was a very fierce golden-furred male bear.

Yōkichi had been attacked by the bear while he was staying in the hut in early autumn three years ago. Yōkichi had been alone. Suddenly in the middle of the night there was a thunderous pounding on the hut door. Yōkichi climbed out of his sleeping bag, wondering what had happened.

He saw that the door had been busted in.

The darkness poured in through the broken door. A large black object loomed in the darkness. It had two small eyes. They flashed briefly in the light of the lantern.

Yōkichi knew it was a bear. He could also see anger in its eyes.

Yōkichi looked for a weapon. There was a hatchet and a gaff hook on the wall of the hut. He ran to get them. As he ran, he shouted at the bear.

Yōkichi had seen the bear several times. Various sea creatures came across the ice floes to the beach by the hut. Sea lions, earless seals, fur seals. In the winter, a variety of marine mammals lived on the Shiretoko Peninsula.

The bear hunted them.

The ice floes started to appear in late January and lasted until March or April. The large sea mammals came and went with them. Bears hibernate in dens during the winter. That's just about the time they come out of their dens. For the first two or three days, they eat butterbur stems and other things while the pads of their paws, which have become soft and tender during hibernation, toughen up again. Then they come to the coast.

One seal or sea lion is quite a feast, even for a large bear.

The seals and sea lions are well aware of the bears and on their guard against them. But the bear persevered, lurking in caves and depressions.

Yōkichi had seen this many times. *It was a very peculiar bear*, he thought. Every bear is different. There are all sorts—bears that hang around the seashore, bears that never leave the mountains, bears that approach human settlements and homes. Once they acquire a certain taste, it becomes a habit. This particular bear must have caught a seal once. Yōkichi felt a little sorry for the bear, and at the same time, thought it was kind of touching, since his quest was so nearly hopeless. It was like some early human standing on a beach looking out at the sea for fish.

That was the bear that had attacked the hut.

It was the beginning of autumn, the season when bears had to try to store as much fat as possible for their upcoming hibernation. But at that time of year there were no seals on the beach. They didn't arrive until winter. Occasionally there might be a stray, but they were especially wary. They would not easily become the bear's prey.

The bear was getting desperate. Its desperation grew into rage. The little eyes of the bear that had forced its way into the hut seemed brutality incarnate. They were burning with aggression.

Yōkichi shouted at the bear. Until this moment he had looked fondly upon the bear. Now the bear was trying to eat him.

Just before he reached the hatchet, the bear struck a blow to Yōkichi's right shoulder. It sent Yōkichi flying.

The blow was incredibly powerful. Yōkichi rolled and tried to escape. But the bear was nimble. The second blow hit his left arm. The bear's claws tore off half the flesh from his arm. Yōkichi thought he was going to die. The next blow came to his head. If it had landed, it would have easily split it open. Then he'd be eaten.

Yōkichi was moving instinctively. He didn't even know what he was doing. When he came to his senses, the bear was on fire.

With flames licking the bear's chest and part of its stomach, it dashed out of the hut.

The lantern lay broken on the floor. Part of the floor was on fire.

Yōkichi crawled to the wall and grabbed the hatchet.

He was fifty-eight years old at the time.

Five days later, in the hospital, he had his left arm amputated at the shoulder.

Yōkichi hated the bear.

He'd decided to kill it.

He had thought of the bear as a kind of fellow fisherman. They were both homeless sojourners, looking to the sea to provide them with a certain modest sustenance. There was no need to fight with each other. That's what he'd always thought—up to now. But the bear had directed his anger at not finding any food at the fisherman. Eating the fisherman would fill his belly, he thought.

To Yōkichi, it felt like a betrayal.

No one was going to eat *him*.

A fisherman has his pride, too.

After his arm healed, he started to look for the bear. His weapon was a large lance. He made it himself, heating iron and pounding it. He had sharpened the double-edged blade. The shaft was made of oak and was twelve feet long.

Every autumn, he came to the beach in his boat and waited for the bear.

Three years had passed without him ever encountering it again.

But Yōkichi didn't give up.

That's why he had come to the abandoned hut.

He dragged his boat ashore on a strip of beach quite a distance from the hut and walked up the shore.

It snowed on and off.

When he had come close to the hut, Yōkichi stopped.

What he saw was very strange.

There was a seal on the beach. For a seal to be here out of the ordinary season was not such a strange sight. A cat and a dog were next to the seal. It was a medium-sized dog. It was very thin, and it was lying down next to the seal. The cat was crouched on a rock next to it.

I must be dreaming, Yōkichi thought. He saw an Ezo red fox near the cat.

This was an impossible scene.

Cats and dogs can become friends. But he'd never heard of a dog and a fox, or a cat and a fox, being friends. And the seal lying down in front of the other three—that was inconceivable.

Yōkichi tapped himself on the head.

Yes, he was awake.

In a sort of daze, he watched the animals.

Eventually the seal began to crawl forward. As it did, the dog and the fox ran around it. The cat remained on the rock, merely shifting the direction it was looking. Soon the dog and the fox began playing. The seal lay still again, watching them.

Yōkichi noticed smoke rising from the hut.

He began walking.

What he saw when he looked inside made him open his eyes in surprise.

At first he thought it was a ghost. A pale figure was in the corner of the hut. It was thin. Its skin looked dead. It was green. There was no hair on its head.

It was only after some time that he realized it was a woman. She spoke first. Who are you, she asked. It was the voice that told him it was a woman.

Yōkichi entered the hut.

There were just the barest minimum of necessities.

A pile of driftwood sat next to the stove.

Yōkichi introduced himself.

The woman said her name was Irako Nakase. Her voice was lifeless and hoarse. Yōkichi realized that she was dying. He grasped that when he saw her fingernails. They were colorless. They were long, untrimmed, and split. She seemed to be suffering from extreme malnutrition. Her wrists were like thin bamboo sticks.

Not knowing what to ask, Yōkichi looked at the kitchen. It was next to the room with the stove and the board floors.

There was a small amount of rice and miso. A little dried fish. Nothing else. Empty whiskey bottles lay sidewise on the floor.

There were containers that looked like animals' food bowls on the floor.

Irako sat on a straw mat and leaned against the wood wall of the hut. A sleeping bag was next to her. There was an earth-floored room and a room with a bunk bed, but there was nothing in either space. It was an extremely desolate scene.

"What on earth..." That was all Yōkichi said. He piled several pieces of driftwood in the stove, which was on the verge of going out.

"I'm sorry for using this hut without asking," apologized Irako.

"That's not important. But what's going on here?" Yōkichi sat next to the stove.

"I'm waiting to die," said Irako with a faint smile.

"That's what I thought, but..."

Her eyes were clear. They were large and moist. Her sight seemed to be fading.

"Don't ask me anything, just let me die. Nothing can be done."

"Even if you went to a hospital?"

Irako nodded slightly.

"I see..."

Yōkichi was silent.

Irako had already given her body over to death. Yōkichi could see that.

The dog came in. There was a hole in the wall in a corner of the earthen-floored room. The dog entered from there. Seeing Yōkichi, the dog wagged its tail. It looked like a mix of an Ainu dog and something else. The dog welcomed Yōkichi and then walked over to Irako.

It licked her face. Then it licked her lips. Irako wearily stretched out her arm and hugged the dog around the neck.

Next the cat came in, meowing. The cat walked right up to Irako. Like the dog, it licked Irako's fingers. Its short round tail, like a fist, twitched.

The fox came in. The fox stayed in the earthen-floored room. With its narrow, needle-like pupils it looked at Yōkichi and sat there motionless.

"You're hungry, aren't you?" Irako picked up the cat.

"The cat, the dog, and the fox. And the seal..." What was going on with them, asked Yokochi.

"I don't know," replied Irako, shaking her head slightly.

She really didn't.

She hit the cat with her car on the way to the hut. She stopped her car. She thought she could prevent the detective following her from discovering her whereabouts if she hid the cat's body. In fact, no detective was following her. Irako was the victim. But at the time, she felt as if she could even hear the footsteps of the detective on her tail.

The cat had been alive. She decided to kill it. She picked up a stick to kill it and throw it away. She remembered striking it several times. It looked dead. Then she did something that she didn't understand. She picked up the cat and went back to the car.

Later she asked herself why she picked it up, but she wasn't able to explain it. She had lost her mind, she thought. When she came back to her senses she was in the hut treating the cat's injuries.

By that time she already had no desire to get rid of the cat. She nursed it attentively. For some reason she was afraid that if the cat died, her own life would be snuffed out. She only had a little more than a month to live. After being fully exposed to cobalt radiation, your days were numbered. Though it varied slightly from individual to individual, the difference wasn't more than a week. Death was inevitable and inescapable. Hospitalization would achieve nothing. The only thing they could do was to give you a glucose drip. That was no comfort. Irako knew that she had about forty days, more or less, before her life came to an end.

That time, brief as it was, was better than dying tomorrow. If she were dying tomorrow, she would have no time to think about anything. She'd be too panicked and simply die in terror and distress.

After four days, the cat was able to walk with its splint. It recovered with amazing speed. While it did so, Irako spent the entire day watching it. When she wasn't looking at the cat, she was looking at the Sea of Okhotsk.

Once the cat could walk, she thought that it would leave the hut. Irako had beat it with a stick after she hit it with her car. The cat must have felt her intense intent to kill it. It must have been the cat of someone living in Utoro. It could be back home in two days.

But the cat didn't attempt to leave the hut when it was able to walk again.

It rubbed up against her legs. As it did so, it occasionally mewed. When Irako left the hut, it left the hut. When she walked up to the shoreline, the cat did, too. It was an insoluble mystery to Irako.

When she stood on the beach, the cat climbed a nearby rock and sat crouched there. It watched Irako with its golden eyes. At first she thought that the cat might be planning its revenge. That was the impression she got when she looked in its eyes. They glowed with an ineffable golden light cloaked in mystery. It gave Irako the creeps.

But after several days, that feeling disappeared. The sense of suspicion disappeared from the cat's eyes. There never had been any suspicion in the cat's eyes; it had existed entirely in Irako's mind. The day the suspicion disappeared, Irako picked up the cat. The cat remained still and allowed it. Its furry body was warm. She could feel the softness of its flesh and the pulsing of its life in her hands. She hugged it and was glad she hadn't killed it.

That evening, a dog appeared from somewhere. It was a large, light-colored dog. It sat on the beach looking at the hut.

The cat looked at the dog.

The cat approached the dog, making high-pitched sounds. Watching, Irako was worried. She was afraid the dog would kill the cat. She called loudly to the cat to come back, but it didn't. It walked up to the dog, flicking its short tail.

Irako picked up a stone.

She had a terror of dogs that far surpassed mere aversion. Every dog that had ever seen Irako up to then bared its fangs at her. But those dogs had been on the other side of a fence, or on a leash. The dog before her now was not leashed. If she approached, she was sure that it would not only bare its fangs but viciously attack her.

The cat walked to within several meters of the dog and then stopped. It continued mewing. The dog was wagging its tail. The cat was twitching its short tail, too. They seemed to be talking to each other. Eventually, the dog stepped forward. The cat stayed where it was. The dog placed its nose against the cat. As if it had been waiting for that, the cat turned around.

The cat led the dog back to the hut.

Irako dropped the stone.

She crouched down.

Pain ran through every bone in her body. Her bones were creaking. They were crying out. It seemed her joints would break.

She had been taking morphine pills, but they couldn't relieve such intense pain. She put an aspirin in her mouth. Up to now, most of the illnesses she'd contracted could be cured by aspirin. Aspirin was the most effective remedy for her.

But nothing was a match for the pain she was in now.

It was the second week since she'd been irradiated. Her symptoms were progressing in the precise sequence she'd been taught in her class on radiation therapy. About seventy percept of the hair on her head had fallen out. And not only on her head. Her pubic hair was also gone. She was gradually turning into a corpse.

Irako rolled on the ground. As she was writhing and calling out in pain, she lost consciousness.

When she came to again, the dog was licking her face. The pain was gone. She was afraid that if she moved suddenly, it would bite her. She remained still. The cat was nearby, mewing. It sounded sad. It made Irako cry. She had remained in the darkness a long time after she lost consciousness. It was absolute blackness. It seemed to her that the cat's voice calling to her had reached her through that blackness. She realized the cat had called her back to life.

Irako stood up. The dog cocked its head and looked at her. It had clear, deep eyes. She sensed no trace of wariness in the dog. "You must be hungry," she said to it.

The darkness of night drifted in from the Sea of Okhotsk and enveloped the beach, and now it was doing the same to the hut. Irako lit the lantern and fed some driftwood into the stove. She made rice. She opened some canned fish, mixed it with the rice, and gave it to the cat and the dog. They ate side by side.

As she watched them, Irako began to cry again. Her tears fell without end, one after another. She couldn't understand why this cat and dog liked her. This shouldn't be. Irako had hated cats, dogs, birds—all living things. She'd killed numerous cats and dogs. And yet, this cat and this dog liked her.

She didn't understand. And not understanding, she wept.

She had only some twenty days to live. She decided that she would keep feeding this cat and dog as long as she lived. She'd brought enough food to last for forty days. The dog, if not the cat, would need a large amount of food. *I don't care*, thought Irako.

As my death approaches, I won't have any appetite anyway. Even now, she ate only one meal a day, if she ate at all.

That night strong gusts of wind assaulted the beach. A winter gale whistled all night. The hut shook, and the wind blew in through its cracks, wailing even inside it. It was an extremely desolate feeling. A dreadful wind battered Irako's heart.

The cat and the dog slept next to the stove. That sight also brought tears to Irako's eyes. If she'd been alone, she would have gone insane with sadness, she thought.

The wind had stopped by morning.

Irako awoke late. When she did, neither the cat nor the dog were there. She went outside. The sea was still rough from the wind of the night before. There was foam on the beach. She saw no sign of either the cat or the dog on the shore.

She crouched in the doorway. She realized that the cat and the dog had left the hut together. She hadn't the energy to even whisper to herself. She felt as if her internal organs has disappeared. There was no weight at all in her stomach. Her legs were shaking.

She crouched there for some time. Her eyes watching the sea were dim. She had lost about half her eyesight from the radiation. She tried to stand, and started coughing. She coughed several times and spit up phlegm. It was bright red. The blood fell on the driftwood, bleached as white as bones.

Irako looked at it. A part of her oral mucous membrane was mixed in with the phlegm. It must have come off when she was coughing. Her teeth were loose. She tried biting down, and her teeth sunk down as if they were set soft clay.

She looked to the sea.

They've gone, she thought.

She turned and hobbled back to the hut.

The cat and dog had still not returned at night.

Irako took morphine, aspirin, and an iron supplement all together, and slipped into her sleeping bag.

She didn't fall asleep until morning.

She had a dream, which woke her up. It was a dream about being irradiated with the cobalt. Her weakened heart was beating as if it would burst. She looked blankly up at the ceiling. The lantern, dirty with soot, cast a dim light. In it, she relived the scene in the radiotherapy room.

Dr. Shimada had approached her. He'd called her first. He said he was lonely now that his wife and son were dead and asked if she'd be interested in getting together with him. Irako replied that she'd like to think about it. Several days later, they met in the radiotherapy room at night. Irako let him kiss her. She was prepared, naturally, to have sex with him. She let him get on top of her and didn't resist, giving herself to him. He undressed her and embraced her on the floor. Irako liked Shimada. But Shimada had never shown any interest in her. She thought that at last she had him.

After intercourse, they parted.

After Irako returned to the nurse station, she was overcome by a terrible headache. She felt like vomiting. She was dizzy, as if seasick. Still, it didn't occur to her that she had radiation poisoning. She took some medicine that the doctor on duty gave her. That's when she got the phone call from Shimada. He told her that he'd opened the valve on the radiation machine, releasing cobalt radiation for about an hour before they went into the room. He laughed in a deep, heavy voice.

"We're both going to die," he said.

That's the moment that appeared in her dream. It was a terrifying dream. She'd had it several times. It didn't seem so much that she was dreaming it as that it was imprinted on her mind, replaying itself.

Irako closed her eyes.

When she opened them again, the sun was up. She thought she heard the cat somewhere. She crawled outside. She saw an unbelievable sight. The cat was sitting on a piece of driftwood mewing. The dog and a red Ezo fox were running around the driftwood. At first she didn't think it was a fox. She thought it was another dog, a friend of the big one. But it was unmistakably a fox. It had yellowish brown fur. Its face was narrow and its muzzle pointed. And the tail was long, its body thin.

Irako watched in astonishment.

Foxes are common on Shiretoko Peninsula. Many of them are accustomed to tourists. They come out to the roads to take food from people. They wait for people to toss scraps to them. Irako knew that. But she'd never heard of a fox and a dog playing together. Dogs are the natural enemies of foxes. They're both in the same canine family, but they hate each other.

The sight of a dog and a fox playing together was quite extraordinary.

As she watched, the cat came up to her, mewing.

The cat rubbed against Irako's legs. Irako picked it up. She looked at its eyes. A bewitching light seemed to shine from them. Irako felt a chill run through her. *This is no ordinary cat*, she thought. She had killed several cats by dousing them with boiling water. She felt as if this cat had come to take revenge upon her for her deeds. Irako was overcome with a fear that it was some kind of demon cat.

Irako flung the cat away, throwing it down. It flew through the air and landed on its feet on the floor. It looked up at Irako and mewed. Continuing to mew, it sidled up to her, rubbing against her. Irako pressed her back against the wall. Sinking down to the floor, she implored it in a pitiful voice not to come near, to go away, to forgive her.

But the cat didn't go away. It stood right in front of her, mewing and looking at her. It continued its mewing. Irako put her hands over her ears. The cat's retaliation had begun. "You killed my friends, and now I'm going to avenge them," it said. "I brought a dog. I brought a fox. I'm going to bring more and more animals. And then we'll take our vengeance."

"I'm sorry!" shouted Irako, weeping.

Her shout sent her into a bone-breaking spasm. She fell over, writhing on the floor. She thrashed wildly in pain. She jerked up and down like a shrimp. Blood flowed from her mouth, now without a mucous membrane. Her loosened teeth pushed into the flesh of her gums.

Eventually she lost consciousness.

When she awakened, the dog was licking her face. Its tongue was warm. It was wet with saliva, the proof of life.

The cat was sitting by the stove.

The fox was in the earth-floored entryway. It was looking at Irako with a puzzled expression, as if wondering what had happened to her. She could hear the sound of the waves. There was the sound of the wind, too. The waves and wind intensified the silence. The hut was immersed in the utter desolation of winter on Shiretoko, a desolation that would turn a person's heart to stone.

Irako softly squeezed the dog's leg. The dog licked her hand. She felt no malice or threat in it. It was an affectionate lick.

The cat mewed again.

The cat's voice made Irako realize that the cat, the dog, and the fox were hungry. For some reason, she clearly understood that they were asking to be fed, and quickly. She slowly got up. They were depending on her. She roused herself, determined to take care of the cat, the dog, and the fox.

Several days passed.

The fox showed no sign of returning to the woods. It spent its days playing with the dog. It gradually grew accustomed to Irako. Little by little it became comfortable approaching her, until eventually it would take food from her hand.

Irako's weakness intensified. At the beginning of the fourth week since her radiation exposure, blood began to appear in her urine. Ulcers appeared over her body, both internally and externally, and bled. She had a week, or at most, ten days left to live.

A little after noon, the cat was outside mewing. It sounded different than usual. Using a piece of driftwood as a cane, Irako went outside.

A large seal was on the beach. The cat was approaching it, mewing. Its tail, like an infant's fist, twitched this way and that. The seal raised its head and looked at the cat.

Irako stood watching the scene.

Clearly, the cat was trying to befriend the seal. The dog and the fox weren't there; apparently they'd gone off into the woods. The cat had used the same approach to befriend the dog. No doubt it had also been the cat who added the fox to the little circle of companions, too. Now it was trying the same thing with the seal. Irako watched breathlessly, wondering what its magic was.

The cat stopped right in front of the seal. The seal looked down at the cat. It was prepared to attack at the first aggressive motion.

A cat was no threat to its life; it seemed, rather, to be observing the animal.

The cat mewed. It kept mewing, as if it was saying something. The seal remained motionless. The cat, still mewing, moved around to its side. The seal moved. The cat moved. The cat was clearly much nimbler. Walking around and around, the cat touched the seal with its front paw. Then it shook its paw several times, as if surprised by what it felt.

The seal barked. It seemed impatient with the cat's quickness and its constant mewing. Still barking, it pushed off into the water. But it didn't swim away. It stayed near the shore, its head above the water. The cat climbed up on a rock and mewed toward the seal's face. The seal looked suspiciously at the little insistently crying creature.

Eventually the seal swam away.

The cat, appearing disappointed, began to lick its paws, still sitting on the rock. Irako smiled wryly and went back into the hut. She realized it was neither a magic nor a demon cat. It was a curious cat. That was all there was to it. The dog and the fox possessed a curiosity equal to that of the cat, and the three of them just happened to encounter each other. The disappointed way the cat licked its paws when the seal deserted it was funny.

From the next day, Irako stayed in bed.

She ate almost nothing for several days in succession. Her hands and feet became so thin that they looked like birds' feet.

Scale-like cracks began to appear in her skin. It didn't bother her to look at them. She had no narcissism left, of course. All that she had left now was a tranquility, awaiting the death that would come to her in a few more days.

She remained in bed day and night. Death's massive talons were already inside the hut. She could feel their presence. But strangely, she wasn't afraid. She wasn't upset by dying. She was simply waiting.

When she left Tokyo, she'd brought drugs from the hospital to kill herself with. They would have killed her instantly. As she made her way to Shiretoko, she was depending on those drugs. She would take them at the last moment. Soon she'd be at peace. There was no cure for the radiation exposure she'd undergone.

She could weep and wail as much as she liked, but death would come to her, without fail. Her hair would fall out, her mucous membranes would slough off, her teeth and nails would crumble until they were powder. She didn't want anyone to see her dying like that. Dr. Shimada would die, too. She was afraid that before he did, he'd tell the police that he'd taken his revenge on Irako. She didn't want the police to chase after her, catch her, and put her into a hospital as she underwent this miserable death.

She came to the hut on Shiretoko because she wanted to die alone.

Her trip there was filled with the fear of death, her remorse at her own nature, and her hatred for Shimada. She didn't try to think about anything. If she had, her head would have burst. She was already in a state of intense stress. She was afraid she might lose her mind, and if that happened, she wouldn't be able to regain control, she thought. She was prepared to die insane in the desolation of the abandoned hut.

She intended to take the fatal drug before she lost her mind.

But now she felt no fear, no remorse, no hatred. She no longer intended to rely upon a drug that would bring the curtain down on her life. The cat had extinguished the fear in her heart. The dog had slowly and steadily taken away her sadness and attachment to life.

The only thought left in her mind was the worry of who would care for the cat and the dog after she'd died. The fox could return to the woods. But the cat and the dog would still be hungry the day that Irako died.

That was her only worry.

Aside from that, her heart was clear.

She remained on the floor, waiting for death.

It was all she could manage to give the cat, the dog, and the fox their food in the morning and the evening.

Two days after she'd taken to her bed, her sight dimmed drastically. She could only make out the blurry forms of the cat and the dog.

She could still hear. She could still hear the waves, the wind, the cat's mewing, and the dog's barking.

Irako enjoyed listening to those sounds.

Yōkichi Kitami was walking along the beach, using his long lance as a stick.

As before, the seal, the dog, the cat, and the fox were playing on the sand. The cat sat on a rock above the others, their leader. The seal was barking sharply and moving about, tossing up small stones. The dog was chasing the fox around him. Just when it seemed the dog would catch him, the fox would leap up like a brown bird to a high rocky perch. The dog would twist its body as it leaped up to try to reach it, but fall back down. Then the seal would try to climb the rocks.

The cat watched all this, mewing in a piercing voice.

Yōkichi watched these goings on as he walked.

Irako didn't know that the cat had succeeded in befriending the seal. She didn't know that, after leaving, the seal had returned.

It was starting to snow.

7

The kelp harvester's hut on the beach facing the Sea of Okhotsk sat quietly under a blanket of snow.

Detective Tokuda arrived at the hut in Yōkichi Kitami's boat.

The beach was silent. There was no trace of any life.

When he stepped off the boat onto the shore, Tokuda realized that Irako Nakase was dead. Yōkichi Kitami had seen her at the hut four days earlier. According to Yōkichi, it looked liked she had only a few days left to live.

He'd said that a dog, a cat, a fox, and a seal had been playing on the beach. There was no sign of any of the creatures there now. Both the beach and the hut were devoid of life.

He walked with Yōkichi up to the hut.

"The bear," said Yōkichi softly, holding Tokuda back with his right arm.

There were bear tracks in the snow. They went up to the hut. Yōkichi saw that the door to the hut had been broken in.

Tokuda pulled out his gun.

Tokuda went ahead of Yōkichi toward the hut. Snow had fallen in through the broken door and lightly dusted the earthen-floored entryway. Imagining Irako's half-eaten corpse, Tokuda stepped in.

Irako lay on the floor of the rush-matted living room. She was dead, curled up like a shrimp. Her hands were stretched out in front of her. This is what you look like when you die struggling with pain. Her clear eyes were open.

Tokuda looked silently at her body.

It was as cold as one of the stones on the beach.

There were no traces of an attack by the bear.

Her wasted form was shrunken in on itself like a little demon. She had no hair. Her frozen little head looked like that of a young boy.

Tokuda stepped out of the hut.

Yōkichi, who had been studying the bear's tracks, stood next to him.

"The bear attacked the hut. During the day, yesterday. But the dog drove the bear off. The fox and the cat fought it, too. The tracks of all three of them fighting bravely are here." Yōkichi spoke softly.

"I see," said Tokuda, nodding and walking toward the shore.

He hunched down in the sand and took out a cigarette.

Having seen Irako's corpse, Tokuda could calculate roughly when she died. It appeared it had been about two days ago. If the bear had attacked yesterday, the dog, the cat, and the fox had watched over Irako's corpse for a full day.

Then they'd gone away.

Yōkichi crouched next to him.

The rough sea was dark and heavy. The horizon blended in with the low clouds hanging over it.

Yōkichi was silent.

So was Tokuda.

On the surface of the sea, Tokuda envisioned the sight of the cat, the dog, the fox, and the seal playing, as described by Yōkichi. Irako had hit the cat with her car. She beat it wildly with a stick to kill it, but then she changed her mind and nursed it back to health. For some reason, the cat then came to like Irako.

The cat brought the dog, the fox, and even a seal that had appeared unseasonably on the beach, into a little band of friends.

This was impossible, thought Tokuda. Foxes and dogs don't get along, and cats and dogs don't usually, either. The same was true of cats and foxes. The idea of adding a seal to this mix was absolutely inconceivable.

What brought these four beings together?

Was it the cat, he asked himself. No. It may have been the cat or the dog who created this friendship among the four animals in the abandoned hut at the end of the world, but what must have caused them to do this strange thing, he believed, was Irako. It seemed to him that the cat, the dog, and the fox, and finally the seal, had created a little ring of friendship here on the deserted beach, with Irako in the center.

Without Irako, the cat wouldn't have come to the hut. The same was true of the dog and the fox. The seal might have arrived at the abandoned beach, but it would have very soon swum off again.

He thought of Irako's corpse, now a little demon.

"A sacred demon," he said to himself.

It seemed to him that she had died transformed into a sacred demon creature.

"I," began Yōkichi in a rough voice," I've decided to give up chasing after the bear." That was all he said.

After a moment, Tokuda nodded.

Tokuda didn't know why Yōkichi had decided not to kill the bear. He didn't understand, but he thought it was the right thing to do.

It seemed to him that it was wrong to kill a living thing, for whatever the reason.

The town of Utoro sits on two sides of a narrow road. The road is bumpy. The bumps had been smoothed over with snow. There are rarely any cars driving down the road. The wind blew through the town in a kind of wind tunnel. Broken by the fishing nets on the seaside edge of the town, the wind whistled low.

A white dog and a brown cat were walking down the road from east to west.

A black dog in the town barked at them. It tried to attack the cat, running up to them. Before the cat could defend itself, the white dog turned around. It threw its body into the black dog It was all over in a minute. The black dog ran off howling.

The white dog and the brown cat continued walking together down the road.

There was no sign of people.